Dear Reader,

As a child, "The Twelve Dancing Princesses" was a favorite story of mine—so magical! Beautiful princesses escape the shackles of their lives each night, and dance in an ethereal fairyland to their hearts' content until dawn.

The Princess He Must Marry puts a multicultural twist on this beautiful old story. Nigeria, where my heroine Tobi is from, has an enduring tradition of kingships and chieftaincies. States, towns and villages often have kings (or, *obas*, in the Yoruba language) who contribute much to their local communities.

Tobi is the second daughter of the *oba* of a small fictional town just outside Badagry, a real-life coastal city in Lagos State. Like her counterparts in the fairy tale, she escapes from under the eye of a domineering father. In doing so, Tobi connects her older sister, Kemi, with the love of her life (*The Royal Baby He Must Claim*) and marries a North African prince of her own in this story!

I hope you enjoy this twist on the fairy tale, and love Tobi and Akil as much as I do.

Happy reading,

Jadesola

Jadesola James loves summer thunderstorms, Barbara Cartland novels, long train rides, hot buttered toast and copious amounts of cake and tea. She writes glamorous escapist tales designed to sweep you away. When she isn't writing, she's a university reference librarian. Her hobbies include collecting vintage romance paperbacks and fantasy shopping online for summer cottages in the north of England. Jadesola currently lives in the UAE. Check out what she's up to at jadesolajames.com!

Books by Jadesola James

Harlequin Presents

Redeemed by His New York Cinderella

Jet-Set Billionaires
The Royal Baby He Must Claim

Carina Press

The Sweetest Charade

Visit the Author Profile page
at Harlequin.com for more titles.

Jadesola James

THE PRINCESS HE MUST MARRY

If you purchased this book without a cover you should be aware
that this book is stolen property. It was reported as "unsold and
destroyed" to the publisher, and neither the author nor the
publisher has received any payment for this "stripped book."

Recycling programs
for this product may
not exist in your area.

ISBN-13: 978-1-335-58359-8

The Princess He Must Marry

Copyright © 2022 by Jadesola James

All rights reserved. No part of this book may be used or reproduced in
any manner whatsoever without written permission except in the case of
brief quotations embodied in critical articles and reviews.

This is a work of fiction. Names, characters, places and incidents
are either the product of the author's imagination or are used fictitiously.
Any resemblance to actual persons, living or dead, businesses,
companies, events or locales is entirely coincidental.

For questions and comments about the quality of this book,
please contact us at CustomerService@Harlequin.com.

Harlequin Enterprises ULC
22 Adelaide St. West, 41st Floor
Toronto, Ontario M5H 4E3, Canada
www.Harlequin.com

Printed in U.S.A.

THE PRINCESS HE
MUST MARRY

To my little ones, who make the writing process both a challenge and a joy! I love you dearly, and I look forward to seeing your own happy endings someday.

CHAPTER ONE

Badagry, Nigeria

IT WAS TIME for the bride to dance in, and despite the ruby-encrusted stilettos she was very precariously balanced on, Princess Tobilola Obatola felt as if she were floating. Her vision was partially obscured by a gossamer-light veil, shot through with threads of actual gold.

She had no worry in stepping forward; her attendants were all there, perfumed in a custom blend of rosewater and lemon that made them a fragrant, powdered, gold-draped mass of moving bodies. There were two at her back and one at each elbow, ready to guide the former princess of Gbale—and future princess of the royal principality of Djoboro—to her place at her husband's side. The *álágás,* traditional emcees who were also there to playfully hustle money for the bride from her husband's family, who had come prepared with full purses, were making quite the show of it, and their voices boomed directly into Tobi's ear from a too-loud speaker.

"Our bride, the daughter of His Majesty the Oba of Gbale, His Esteemed Greatness, is here to honor our gathering—"

Tobi barely managed to suppress a giggle. Even on his daughter's wedding day, her father ensured he was recognized. Through the veil, her eyes connected to the warm brown ones of her older sister, Kemi, who shot her a warning look, though it was tempered by a smile.

Behave, she mouthed. Tobi lifted her chin and tossed her head in answer, setting the heavy rubies set in gold dancing in her ears. Oh, she would behave today. That was for certain.

The *bàtá* musicians held their hourglass-shaped *dùndún* drums tight beneath their arms and began to play an enticing rhythm, intended to draw her and her bridesmaids forward. Tobi mixed the shy mincing steps of a modest bride with the swaying hips and waist of a seasoned woman, moving forward lightly, flicking her wide fan open so that it glittered and ruby-studded streamers fell neatly to the ground.

The head *álágá,* sweating beneath her impressive *gele* headdress, announced Tobi's arrival in playful Yoruba, entreating the guests to welcome her, and her husband's family to shower her with gold. Beside her, her translator swayed, interpreting her words for the foreign guests.

"Dance, our bride, dance well—"

The room was awash in laughter and applause and the slightly giddy sounds of champagne-soaked celebration, and as Tobi danced, there was only one thought in her head.

I've pulled this off! I'm free!

Free from her domineering father. Free from a life under virtual lock and key, interrupted only by whatever acts of rebellion she'd been able to manage, bribing guards with jewelry, sneaking out to dance the night away...

Memories faded into reality as she made her way across the massive hall. Somewhere in the corners of her consciousness, she took in the details that featured in any traditional Yoruba high society wedding: round tables, laden with centerpieces of rubies, roses and gold-leaf-plated flatware; the elegantly hand-embroidered *aso ebe* worn as uniform by the members of the royal family; the cell phones and tablets held aloft to capture a glimpse of the royal bride; and finally her princely husband and his entourage, waiting for her, draped in glossy robes of the deepest ruby red.

The only one that mattered, really, Prince Akil Al-Hamri, her husband, led the pack, flanked at the elbow by his brother, Prince Malik.

They were both softer casts of their father, King Al-Hamri the Third, who sat imperiously on a miniature version of the great throne he used in Djoboro. The tiny North African principality hugged the coast of Morocco. It was created, legend had it, by descendants of Mansa Musa who had defected from his hajj caravan centuries ago, made it slowly and perilously across the desert in search of the sea, and set up a settlement. You could see the mark of their Malian ancestors in the proud tilt of their chins, full mouths, and gently tinted skin, a shade or two deeper than their Moroccan neighbors, although centuries of intermarriage had created a diversity that was nothing short of stunning.

Akil, Tobi thought, mouth suddenly growing dry, was a perfect representation. Then she shook herself severely. You'd think at nearly twenty-one years, she'd be able to relegate childhood crushes to where they belonged—between the locked covers of old Disney princess diaries.

She finally reached the dais with the men.

Tobi knew her part without any prompting from either her sister or the *alaga ikoro*, who was eager to move the ceremony along. She knelt before her father, closed her eyes as he murmured prayers over her. Her stepmother was next, the woman's voice low and cultured, as she'd tried without success for years to replicate in Tobi.

The king of Djoboro's prayers were concise but heartfelt, and at the end he lifted her chin, peering at her through the veil.

"I am thrilled," he said, in a voice loud enough to carry through the hall, "that our homes will be so united. The oba of Gbale has been a friend since we were schoolboys, and to have our children find happiness together is one of the great joys of my old age."

Then it was over, and Tobi lowered herself before her husband. The marble floor of the dais burned hard and cold through the fine beaded fabric of her *iro*.

She glanced up through the veil, only for a second. The look on Akil's face was stoic, although there was a glimpse of conspiracy there that danced round his mouth in the form of a smile. His long fingers moved to grasp the edge of her veil, lifting it gently over her head.

The assembly sighed as one.

"We pulled it off," he said through his teeth, then cleared his throat and launched into his own blessing. Wishes for health, longevity, children—

Her face burned. Things that were not to be for them, as they'd be divorced as soon as they could manage. Her husband had married her to get an inheritance; she'd married him to gain her freedom. There was to be no marital bliss, no happy ending at the end of this fairy tale. There would be no point in looking upon her husband with favor; they would never be together, not in that way. It didn't matter that he was tall and sinewy, with broad shoulders and a tapered, dimpled chin that would have looked utterly absurd had he not been so…large, capable, assured. There was no reason to picture what those arms around her might feel like, or—

There was no time to think; Akil had finished speaking. She took the ceremonial cap of marriage in her hand, placed it on his head with trembling hands. Then there were exchanges of books of faith, of rings, and they stood and turned to face a cheering crowd, thrilled because at last they could dance, and eat.

She was married.

More importantly, she was free.

"Hell of a way to spend a wedding night, little brother."

Akil blinked, startled out of the reverie he'd been in for the past hour or so. The massive suite of the villa rented and renovated for the express purpose of housing the king of Djoboro and his guests was virtually empty; most of his groomsmen, Djoboran mates from school and otherwise, had taken a chartered plane to Lagos to get drunk and prowl the nightclubs for women, he supposed.

Akil had other plans.

"Why aren't you with the boys?" he countered, turning his back on his older brother and placing two shirts into an overnight case. Normally a servant would do the packing, but he needed to be as discreet as possible tonight. A covert flight would be leaving Lagos in the morning, and he needed to be in the airport well before then. Only he and the generously paid pilot of the Djoboran Royal Flyer knew his true destination.

"You know Jamila would end my life if I dared." Malik came up behind Akil, peered over his shoulder; his big brother's extra two inches served him well here. "And you're...planning a runner."

"My plans for the evening are my business."

"Where's your bride?"

He glanced down at his watch. Tobi, presumably in her own chambers, was doing a similar packing job. Their cover story tonight was that they were running away to Lagos under the cover of darkness to leave for a secret honeymoon. In reality, Tobi had purchased her own ticket to Dubai, where she had friends, she said. No one knew that the "lovestruck bride and groom" would be headed to separate destinations.

Akil lifted his head, turned and faced Malik. His brother's face was good-humored, but also slightly suspicious. He'd been confused by Akil's sudden wish to marry, unconvinced by his claim of infatuation with Tobi, and had been trying to connect the dots since then.

Akil, frankly, didn't really care if he did or not.

What his family did meant little to him. His life was finally beginning. He'd planned this escape carefully for the past few years. Exciting new business ventures awaited him, where he'd be able to operate as his own man, not the spare to the throne of Djoboro, his movements not examined through the lens of a throne that would never be his. Spending years under the exasperated gaze of Malik and the king hadn't helped, either. Among other things…some too dark for him to ever utter to Malik. He'd tried once, and he would not reflect tonight on how miserably that had turned out.

Djoboro's gleaming palace hid many dark secrets, including the treatment of its second royal son. And as much as he loved his country— as much as that love for it had kept him there long after it was healthy—the time was finally right, and the thought made his lips twitch as he spoke, deadened his expression.

"She's in her room," he drawled, "packing as well. I think we're entitled to a private getaway after all that drama, yes?"

Malik had the grace to look embarrassed. "Oh."

"Don't worry, the renegade prince has no intent of bolting this time. I won't embarrass you."

"Akil…"

"You know, I think you'd lay off on at least my wedding day." He shot his brother a sardonic smile, then shouldered his bag and headed out into the hall.

He didn't look back.

When Akil finally exited the villa, eager to get some fresh air before being confined for the ride to Lagos, the massive compound was quiet. Even the mosquitoes and other night insects seemed to be exhausted from the night's festivities, and the white stone garden was almost eerily quiet. Akil started when the door behind him opened, and Tobi crept out, only a few feet from where he stood.

"The driver's pulled up outside the gate," she said, but she hesitated. "You're going."

"You are, too." His mouth curved upward. "Dubai, right?"

"Right." Her fingers moved self-consciously to the elaborate wedding coiffure still on her head.

"How are you getting there?"

"Etihad."

"First class, I hope."

Even in the darkness he saw a flash of milk-white teeth. "Thanks to your generosity."

That's right. He cleared his throat. The payout he'd given her was hefty but would be nothing compared to the trust he was to receive. And why, he wondered, did this feel suddenly awkward?

Akil knew her as the daughter of his father's friend, of course. He'd watched her grow up in bursts at events they'd both attended over the years, and his memories of her were mostly as a bewitchingly pretty little girl, one who never stopped talking. He'd been a boy himself and taken little notice of her except for that one fact.

Her rebelliousness had come to light when his father and older brother were discussing her after a visit from the old king, who had complained when asked about his children, who sat with their stepmother, presumably gossiping with the women at their own entertainment that evening.

"Kemi is a good girl, but Tobilola is a trial," he'd said grimly. "I can't wait till she's another man's problem."

The men had laughed good-naturedly, but Akil saw it firsthand when he ran into his underage guest later that night, dressed clearly for Djoboro's rather vibrant nightlife. He'd been eighteen then, so Tobi must have been—fifteen or so? She'd been wearing far too much makeup, a dress he supposed she fancied made her look older, and a scowl that was meant to frighten him off.

"Aren't you supposed to be at the veterans dinner?" she'd demanded before he could ask any questions.

"Aren't you supposed to be in bed with a glass of milk?" He'd been amused, despite himself. Blowing off his princely duties for the evening possibly wasn't the classiest move of the night, but no one ever missed him when Malik was there. Not that this slip of a girl needed to know those details. It was embarrassing enough to have to sneak out of *anywhere* at his age. Tobi, at least, would understand the nuances of respect in African culture; outright defiance was something to be carefully considered, especially for a royal son.

Again, he wasn't going to explain that to *her*.

She narrowed her gaze, and the two eyed each other for a moment, then she slung an obnoxiously bright designer bag over one slim shoulder. "I won't tell if you won't," she announced, clearly pleased with her notion of mutually assured destruction.

Akil's first impulse had been to laugh in her face, but something about her earnestness held him back. He bit back the snort instead. "How do you plan to get out?"

"Taxi. Called it already." She waved a rhinestone-studded phone under his nose.

"Have fun." He'd pushed his hands into his pockets and pushed off, then paused to look over his shoulder. "Oh, and Tobi?"

"Eh?"

"When you get back, have them drop you off at the north gate. Ahmed's the night guard, and he isn't a tattletale."

He'd saluted her half mockingly before leaving.

Now the party princess was his wife, and they were both still running away. Him to be his own man, no longer tethered by the crown, and Tobi? What did she want? Her own freedom, she'd said, with a trace of desperation in her voice. The seed had been planted in his mind only a few years ago, at her older sister Kemi's wedding; the two had been seated near each other and fell into conversation. Tobi's face was especially morose for a bridesmaid, and he'd been just tipsy enough to ask her why.

"I'll miss her," she'd confessed. "It isn't easy, living at the palace."

"Isn't it?"

"My father is very strict." Her lovely face had been troubled, and in that moment, he'd sensed a kindred spirit.

"You'll have to marry then yourself, and get out," he'd said lightly, and her eyes flashed.

"Trust me, I would if I had the chance!" she declared. "It's stupid to even have this conversation in the twenty-first century—"

"Your reality isn't the same as everyone else's," he'd said mildly. "And neither is mine." He'd heard the rumors about her father's strictness with his daughters; everyone had. Conversation had drifted to other matters, but an idea had taken root. And the moment he'd decided to take his wedding inheritance and use it to fund his new life, he'd needed a coconspirator, and Tobi was who he thought of immediately.

So here they were.

There was something very companionable about standing there in the muggy gray darkness with her: there were details he hadn't had the time, or the inclination, to notice before. Unlike the heavy woven fabrics of her bridal set, she now wore a slinky dress that dipped low in the front and barely skimmed her thighs; the way it clung to the soft points of her body was especially distracting.

He felt his body stir, half turned to face her and looked at her, really looked at her, for what felt like the first time.

She's lovely. Large dark eyes, a full mouth, perfect skin, and soft curves that manifested in full breasts and lush hips. She shifted a little and his throat tightened as he caught a glimpse of the dusky points of her nipples, visible through the dress.

Where the hell was she going, dressed like that?

He was startled when Tobi cleared her throat and took a step forward. Her face was unreadable, steeled into a light expression.

"Thank you," she said, and her arms went round him briefly. He heard her clear her throat. She was muttering something else, but Akil was startled by a frisson of lust so powerful he nearly took a step back.

Had he done that he would have completely missed the soft slide of her breasts on his chest, the sweet musk that rose from her skin. She was all warmth and softness, and he was suddenly dizzy, affected by a physical pull so strong it disoriented him for a moment. Yes, he'd seen women in the past and wanted them, almost immediately. Yes, in some ways, the entire night had been set up for this, with all that close, heated contact while dancing, while holding his new bride tight for intimate photos. But this—

Tobi stepped back. He could hear a car pulling up. Instinctively—possessively—his hand slid down to capture her left, drew it up to look at the large cluster of rubies and gold beads on her ring finger.

Embarrassed, she tugged her hand back. "Should I give it—"

He shook his head quickly. "Not until we decide to divorce."

She drew in breath. "I suppose we should talk about that."

She was right, but he didn't want to talk about that. He didn't want to do anything besides indulge the completely unpredicted, irrational want that was making his blood run warm. It was, he realized, affecting her as well. Her breathing had quickened, and she hadn't made a move to step out of the circle of his arms. His fingers inched down to cup her hip and she shivered, then softened against him.

She wants you. He was experienced enough to know it, and she wasn't schooled enough to hide it. He'd seduced a stranger more than once, and yes, in many ways Tobi was a stranger. But she was also his wife, and they had a bargain.

He'd made a vow to let nothing hold him back

from this new life, and an entanglement with the young woman who was now tipping full berry-stained lips up in a clear invitation for a kiss…

You haven't enough self-control to be successful at anything. Thank God Malik was born first.

Harsh words, only a few of many, and they hadn't even been the worst of it.

Akil's arms became like iron. Tobi stepped back, looking embarrassed and more than a little confused. She crossed arms over nipples that now protruded clearly from the dress, even in the darkness—

"I'll give you a lift," he found himself saying, and cleared his voice to eliminate the huskiness that threatened to squeeze it tight.

"A lift?"

"To Dubai." He took another, cleansing breath. "I've got the royal jet, you know. They think you're on it anyway. It makes sense."

"It's out of your way."

He allowed his mouth to curve up slightly, and then slowly, deliberately, he allowed his eyes to flicker over her.

"It's probably a terrible idea," he admitted, "but I feel like celebrating, and you're the only one who could…understand that. Will you come?"

Confusion flashed over her face. But in answer, she gracefully reached down into the designer bag at her feet, pulled out a light sleeveless jacket and tugged it on over her dress.

"Okay," she said, smiling.

CHAPTER TWO

"So, what do you want to do?"

Tobi blinked.

"It's a fair question," Akil said in that dry voice she'd come to associate with him. He lifted his heavy brows up and down. In the dimmed light of the Djoboran Royal Flyer, they looked almost too dark for his angular face. "We could eat, watch a film or sleep. There are accommodations for all three on board."

"I know." She'd also known that her new husband was fabulously wealthy, in a way her own father could not boast, and this method of transport was a clear indication. The jet itself was like nothing she'd never seen before. It was all fragrant leather and gold-trimmed paneling. "It's certainly extravagant."

"I'm looking forward to purchasing my own."

"Purchasing your own…jet?"

"Of course. A businessman of my standing needs reliable transport."

Tobi gaped at him. "Just how much is your inheritance, anyway?"

He frowned slightly. "It's ill-bred to talk about money."

"Even with your own wife?" The awkwardness was dispelling with the lightness of the conversation; Akil had never been so friendly to her before. She supposed it had less to do with her charms and more to do with the fact that he'd gotten his way, but considering they were holed up together for six hours, she'd take what she could get.

Akil began to laugh, a low rumble in his chest that felt strangely intimate. "It's not my inheritance. It's a prince's trust that comes to me—*us*—automatically on marriage to a fellow African of royal blood." His eyes skimmed her face. "There's a bonus if you bear me a son, but I think we can make do with what we have now."

Oh. Heat raced to her face. The kiss that she was almost sure they would have shared earlier still hung between them; it had dissipated with the matter-of-factness of boarding and with their banter, but it seemed her husband could summon the energy with barely a tilt of his smile, and Tobi was many things all of a sudden: too warm, too cold and very aware of how close she was sitting to Akil.

"What do you plan on doing with it?" Tobi asked, her voice barely a squeak.

Akil picked up the remote control of the massive entertainment system and fiddled with it, but he didn't attempt to turn it on. He eyed her as if wanting to gauge her sincerity, then took a breath. The moment of clear self-awareness, almost uncertainty, surprised Tobi as much as it touched her, but when he spoke his voice was clear and confident.

"I'd like to sell the sun." He smiled a little bit at her confusion. "Ra Enterprises, to steal a name from our Egyptian brothers." He cleared his throat, sat up a little straighter. "It's an investment company, specifically in solar power. Some years ago, Morocco began an initiative to switch to and advocate for solar power through the country. It's seen some progress, but…" He trailed off. "I think that myself and my investment will make a huge difference. Just—look at the continent, Tobi. We should be the richest in the world, but the power situation in some countries—"

"You don't have to tell *me*," Tobi responded drily. Nigeria was notorious for its electricity outages and poor supply. There were barely any families, regardless of status or income, who did not find it necessary to have a generator. Mismanagement, of course, was the main culprit, but if what Akil was saying was true—

"People won't have to rely on electricity as much," she said softly.

Akil nodded eagerly. "If Morocco is successful, it can be patented in other countries. You know Djoborans have Malian roots, so that is a huge interest for me. And—"

"Nigeria next, *abeg*," Tobi said, mouth twitching. "I'd love to live somewhere without the smell of diesel choking the air at night."

"You might have to wait a bit. Ideally neighborhoods with little or no access to electricity, whether generator or state-made, would get panels first. It's…" Akil's voice trailed off again, and suddenly Tobi felt quite alone, for he looked so far away.

She felt a stab of longing that had little to do with the crush she'd been nursing for so long, or with his closeness, or with the intimacy of the moment. Akil was leaving, just as she was, but he had—purpose. A plan. She was leaving for—what? Freedom? What would that mean, exactly? Being able to party when she wanted? Moving freely without a guard?

Somehow, the luxury celebratory vacation she'd planned for herself in Dubai with some of the money she was getting paled in comparison and seemed more than a little silly. Ambition had been thwarted completely by her experiences, in a way. All her years under lock and key, she'd lived for the thrill of the moment, for the little pleasures she could steal away. Akil, on the other hand, was leaving with a plan, a *mission*.

What could she possibly offer to the world now that she was free? What was she to do with herself? She almost opened her mouth to share this with Akil, but she closed it against the words. It felt remarkably immature and silly, as if she were indulging in a fit of self-pity brought on by a realization of how self-absorbed she was. And in a quick, determined flash, she thought, *There's no one who's ever been proud of me, but when I get to Dubai, I'm going to make sure I'm proud of myself once this is over.*

Akil lounged back against the sofa, closing his eyes; his thick dark lashes made shadows over his cheekbones.

She swallowed before speaking, plucking at the folds of her skirt. She didn't want the conversation to be over, even after her pause to think. "Surely you could do this without leaving, though?"

When he opened his eyes and looked at her, the gentle camaraderie that had been there was completely gone. "No."

"Surely, the king would want—"

"You know nothing about my father and what he might want." The first flash of anger that had crossed his face was now well controlled, but it burned beneath the surface, and with an intensity that made her swallow. "Djoboro has other interests. And none of them include me."

Tobi pressed her hands to burning cheeks, trying to regain her composure. "Do you hate it very much, then?" she asked, softly.

Akil looked away as if embarrassed by his reaction. When he turned back to her his face was like stone but determinedly light.

"No, I don't, but it is not for me anymore, unfortunately." He glanced away darkly, then shook his head as if clearing the thoughts. He turned back to her and smiled tightly. "Film?" he asked, the earlier moment of intimacy well and truly gone. Tobi crossed her arms over her chest, feeling curiously bereft.

"Fine."

"Are you cold?"

"Not really." She caught her lower lip between her teeth and leaned back, then winced as the elaborate chignon on the back of her head sent hairpins digging into her scalp. Akil noticed at once.

"I don't know how you've been carrying that

thing around on your head all day. Can I help you get it off?"

"It is heavy." The chignon was fastened by a large comb of rubies and gold, a gift from Akil's family, and ruby-tipped hairpins were arranged artfully to supplement the heavy knot of braids at the base of her neck. She'd been paranoid about losing any of the precious jewels in the villa, and so had kept the coiffure, but she supposed that on the royal jet…

Taking her admission as assent, Akil gestured for her to move closer. There was one breathless moment where she felt the warmth of his chest at her back, and then those long, slim fingers were gentle at the base of her neck, in her hair.

"I'll go slowly," he said very low by her ear, and though the words surely were not meant to be as sensual as they sounded, she felt a quiver collect low in her stomach. Akil made little noise as he worked; just a grunt here or there as he pulled one heavy pin out, let it drop to the ebony table in front of them with a clatter, then another, and another.

Tobi closed her eyes for a moment and tried to breathe. Akil regarded a pin between his fingers with some curiosity before putting it down.

"Djoboro," he said mildly, "was founded on rubies. That's why it's in everything. Have you ever heard the story?"

"No," she managed. His warm lips were still far too close to her ear, and his voice had dropped to a low rasp. Was he doing this on *purpose?*

"Mali, as you probably know, was an empire built on gold. When the nomads who founded Djoboro left Mansa Musa and traveled to the shores of Morocco, they prayed to Allah for a fruitful resting place. When they settled, at last, it was at the foot of the mountains—now the Djoboran range—that borders the country, taking shelter there.

"The first few years were arduous." He'd finished removing all the ruby pins, and a small pile of them sat glimmering on the table. "You know how legends go—starvation, despair, prayer for a miracle, some enterprising pilgrim stumbles across something that saves the day. Well, ours stumbled across a cluster of rubies, laid bare by a storm he'd taken shelter from. Mining started in the region, and—well. The wealth of the country was built on it, and it's still the only place in Morocco with even a sign of a ruby. We mine other things as well, a few amethysts and loads of copper, phosphate, other less sexy things. But the rubies are where the story is." There was one moment of hesitation, and when he spoke his voice was tinged with regret for the first time since they'd started the conversation. "It's a beautiful place, Tobi. Don't ever let my experiences make you think less of it. I will miss it very much."

He set down the comb on the table, and Tobi let out a sigh of relief as the long thin braids she'd dressed her hair in for the wedding unraveled, falling nearly to her waist. Normally she wore her thick jet-black hair in an Afro blown round her head like a halo, but she'd wanted something she didn't have to think about in her first few days of freedom. She'd barely noticed Akil's fingers in her hair; his heat, the pleasantly spicy sweetness clinging to his skin and the hypnotic timbre of his voice were as soothing as it was.

His fingers were still in her hair, and had he moved closer? She bit her lip hard, then took a breath, leaned back against his chest. She felt him stiffen for a moment, then loosen completely as he exhaled.

That thing that had hung between them earlier was back, and frankly crackled at the edges.

"I didn't intend to seduce you tonight, Tobilola," he said with a frankness that surprised her, and at the word, there was that familiar quiver, low in her belly. Oh, she wouldn't mind if he tried, and she reckoned they both knew it. She wouldn't mind at all. She could not say this in words, of course, even with her trademark boldness, but she did half turn her head to see if he'd take the invitation he'd rejected before. A pause, and then he captured her lips with his...

She registered softness, a gentle warmth that engulfed her senses. He kissed with the same confidence he did everything else, but it was the unexpected softness that startled her into melting against him. She didn't even bother hiding it; she turned round and pressed herself full against him. The thin dress she wore was worse than wearing nothing at all; it was only a barrier to the feel of him on skin that was suddenly tingling. She knew instinctively that he'd handle her body as gently as his mouth moved against hers, and she wanted it more in this moment than—

He was kissing her more urgently now, and she had to bite back the *please* that was threatening to break forth from her mouth. Arching against him was one thing, begging would be another. His lips skimmed a place on her neck she didn't even know was as tender as it was and—

"Akil," she whispered, knotting her fingers in the fine linen of his shirt, as if he'd vanish if she didn't. The sliver of skin where his shirt-tail met his trousers was far too tempting, and she slipped her fingers upward, felt the muscles tense. His skin was warm and taut and she just

knew, even as her face burned at the thought, that he would taste as good as he smelled. He kissed her almost reverently, and she'd never felt more like a princess in her life…

His princess.

Akil's hands slipped upward to grip her thighs, and Tobi retreated into the softness of the cushions with a half sigh. Despite his gentleness, her mouth felt very swollen now, almost bruised; she had no idea how long they'd been kissing. It wasn't just all lust haze, either; her heart was racing. In this setting, the soft lighting, on her wedding night, surrounded by the sort of riches that most people only dreamed of—it was all so romantic, a manifestation of what had started out as a teenage fancy.

"It's okay," she whispered, and the inhalation of breath that followed lifted her breasts, swollen and aching beneath the thin fabric of her dress. His eyes focused on them for one moment, and they darkened. Then he hardened his jaw.

"Tobi," he said, and his voice was not unkind. "Sit up. I'm sorry, this isn't a good idea at all."

Tobi didn't move. "I—what?"

In answer, he released her thighs and cleared his throat, moving backward himself. He extended a hand to help her up and dumbly, she took it. As soon as she was properly upright

Akil was on his feet, that half-pleasant, inscrutable look from the wedding back on his face.

"I'm sorry," he said simply. "That was wrong."

Tobi opened her mouth to answer—with what she didn't know—but Akil was speaking still.

"We're headed in opposite directions, Tobi. You're my wife, and in a way my partner in this, not some pleasant distraction to celebrate a successful night. This isn't fair to you."

Pleasant distraction? She felt as if she'd been kicked in the gut. "Akil—"

He shook his head. "You'll thank me for not… well, you'll thank me. I'm sure you've got your own plans, as well. A liaison would only complicate things."

Complicate your noble vision, Tobi thought a little bitterly, even knowing she had absolutely no right to think like that, no claims to Akil at all. After hearing his grand scheme Tobi still had not managed to shake off that feeling of aimlessness, and, as open as he'd been, he hadn't even asked her specifically about her own plans, had he? And the kisses they'd just shared, he hadn't been particularly attracted to *her,* other than physically. Tobi was no fool; she'd seen how his eyes had lingered on her breasts earlier. He was content to kiss and touch her, but he'd locked her out the moment any sort of intimacy had entered the conversation.

He doesn't care. Why would he? She'd forgotten what he was to her—the means to an end. Tobi had never registered as anything else. That was all, and a few ill-advised kisses in the soft, secluded light was not enough to change that. She wasn't enough to change that. She'd never been worthy of much attention. Her father had made sure of that, and her favored older sister, kind as she was, hadn't helped.

Again came that surge of determination. She would prove to her father, to Akil, to everyone, that she was more. That she had more to offer. This was the beginning of that. "Sorry," she managed. She was trying for a nonchalant voice, but it came out rather strangled.

"There's nothing to be sorry about." Akil cleared his throat. "I'm going to instruct staff to bring us a meal, and you pick something to watch." He looked down at his watch. "Congratulations, Tobi. Freedom in four hours."

Tobi managed a rather sickly smile, but it slid off her face as soon as he was out of sight.

Freedom, yes. Money, yes. But what on earth was she to do with it?

CHAPTER THREE

Three years later

"I'M *BANNED*?"

The sound of her voice reached a pitch that made heads turn in the arrivals line at Dubai International Airport, but Princess Oluwatobi-lola Obatola Al-Hamri didn't care one bit. Her adversary, a bearded officer dressed in a snug-fitting khaki uniform, looked bored at her outburst. Bored!

"No entry," he barked, sliding her passport back to her and waving the next person over.

This infuriated Tobi even more.

"Come," the officer directed, but Tobi ignored him.

"Let me see," she demanded, leaning over the counter to where she'd just had her eyes scanned. Her rhinestone-encrusted Gucci sunglasses clattered to the floor, but she barely noticed. The white-robed immigration officer leaned back in alarm, then looked to make sure the officer was still there.

"Madam, you cannot come over here—"

"And why not? How is this even *happening*?" Tobi's mind raced through every possibility, still coming up short. Her residence permit was still valid. It had been arranged by the mobility team of *African Society*, the reality show she was set to film in three days. For one month she and other prominent society women from the continent would take up residence in the finest suites at the Chantilly Hotel to be wined and dined by the handsomest, richest men in the Emirates, and hopefully, generate enough drama to become the summer's blockbuster hit.

Tobi was feeling more optimistic than she had in a long time—it had been such a rocky road for her. The first eighteen months of her freedom had been fueled by enthusiasm and adrenaline; she'd enrolled in a business program, worked night and day on a business plan, invested heavily and lost spectacularly. It was so bad that she'd actually contacted Akil on impulse. After all, he was her husband, wasn't he?

She hadn't been able to reach him.

She tried official channels—email, a message through his secretary. She was promised extra funds in a carefully worded letter, and the next moment a large amount of money, wired from

Morocco, had shown up in her account, still with no message, no acknowledgment at all.

That was enough for her to burn with humiliation; Tobi could take a hint, and this one had been applied with all the subtlety of a hand grenade. She'd swallowed her pride, paid her debts, buried the real hurt she felt beneath a fit of industry and turned to the one commodity she had—her face, and her name.

Cultivating a socialite persona in Dubai wasn't difficult at all; the culture was ripe for it, and she already had quite a reputation from the social media accounts she'd kept running during her years of captivity, mostly for her own amusement. This show promised a quarter of a million dirhams in her pocket, and grimly Tobi told herself she would never be ashamed of the path she had taken. It was honestly earned money, and some of the socialites and influencers she met were the most elegant, well-educated women she'd ever known. They certainly weren't stupid enough to lose a veritable fortune in a year.

A quarter of a million, she reminded herself as she signed the contract with a flourish.

Per episode.

Sometimes being married to a prince, regardless of how big an ass he was, paid off. Literally.

And if she felt like she was selling off a little of her soul, well then—so be it.

Now Tobi noted through her shock that the nasty little man was speaking rapidly into a black headset. Two female police officers, swathed in a skirted version of his uniform, came over rapidly.

"Ma'am, you have to come with us," said the older of the two.

"I most certainly will *not,"* Tobi said haughtily, drawing herself up to her full height. She reached for her mobile. "I'm going to call my hosts, and they will sort out this problem immedi—"

"Call whoever you want, it will not help," called the immigration officer from where he lounged at a safe distance. Now that backup had arrived, he seemed almost to be enjoying himself. "You have a ban everywhere in the Gulf Cooperation Council. Maybe a problem with another country."

What?

"We can arrange a flight for you back to Nigeria, ma'am," the second female officer said.

Back to Nigeria? Only literal *steps f*rom entering Dubai? After a vacation of only a week?

Over my dead body.

"That won't be necessary," she said. Unconsciously the crisp voice her father used to ad-

dress his staff crept into her vowels; she did not
bother to correct it, as her older sister, Kemi,
often begged her to do. She gathered her irritation around her as a sustaining force. Someone
was going to hear about this, and they weren't
going to like it when they did. She fixed her
face back into its usual imperious expression
and stalked back out for the long walk of shame
back through the arrivals terminal, flanked by
her new friends.

Were he a man who indulged in any sort of
frivolous emotion, Prince Akil Al-Hamri might
have actually been nervous.

He glanced down at the handmade ruby-studded watch on his wrist and took a deep breath
before taking a sip of the rich, smoky Dalmore
that sat in the bottom of the heavy crystal tum-
bler his attendant had just handed him. He'd
need the fortification before facing his sure-to-
be-furious wife.

Tobi.

Even the thought of the lengths he'd had to
go to get her here tonight was irritating. Why
was she so stubborn? He'd sent several politely
worded letters—at least, he assumed they were
politely worded; he'd had no reason to think his
lawyers would be rude—requesting an audience
with her. They'd reached out by phone, email,

even telegram. No response. The only thing his lawyers had produced was that his messages had been received—and Tobi, from all indications, was deep in debt and flying to Dubai to star in a reality TV show.

Akil forced himself to take a deep breath when he realized he was gripping the glass tight enough to imprint the pattern into his palm. There was a tightening at his temples, too, one that the aspirin he'd taken as a preventative did little to assuage. It wasn't just irritation at the thought of her ignoring him: it was a faint, niggling guilt that was born of what he'd done to her eighteen months ago. She'd reached out for help. He'd ignored her. He'd wanted to drive home the message that their lives were to be completely separate and sent a good chunk of money to get the message across.

You weren't fair to her. And now you want a favor.

It was not the ideal position for him to be in.

He glanced at his watch again; his contact at immigration had confirmed her arrival an hour ago. Plenty of time for his wife to have worked up a good head of steam.

Akil rose to his feet, placed down his glass and headed for the exit.

There was no way in hell he was going to enjoy this, but he had no other choice.

"You *bastard*!"

Akil found Tobi in the lobby of the Dubai International Airport Hotel, a no-frills accommodation with the ugliest striped carpet he'd ever seen in his life. His wife looked completely out of place, shifting from one designer high heel to the other, and he took a long moment to survey her carefully. He hadn't seen her since their wedding night three years ago.

She was dressed in the flamboyant style she'd adopted soon after marriage, no doubt a response to finally escaping from under her conservative father's thumb. The ruched minidress she wore glowed against her smooth dark skin and ended mid-thigh, showcasing strong, slim legs that were perfect stems for the curves above. The neckline was as low as the hem was high, and thin gold chains looped round her slender neck. Despite all her jewelry, she was missing one crucial piece on her left hand, and he raised his brows.

"Where's your ring?" It's not like he could have missed it. The hideous thing had come from the royal vault, and could likely have been seen from space.

She glared, ignoring the question. "I should

have known you were behind this," she fumed.
The anger on her face did nothing to diminish
her beauty. It was the first thing that Akil had
noticed about her on their wedding day, to be
honest, after all those years apart. The full lips
in the round face and heavily lashed, doll-like
eyes still gave her a look of innocent prettiness,
despite the layers of makeup she wore. He cast
his eyes down to the Louis Vuitton carry-on
luggage at her feet, as well as the various bags
from duty-free, bulging with purchases.

"You really left me no choice, Tobi. I've been
trying to reach you, and you didn't reply." He
gestured that she should sit in one of the leather
chairs in the hotel lobby. She sank down into
the nearest one; he suspected she needed to,
and fought back a sudden urge to smile. Nothing about this was funny, but seeing Tobi so
ruffled was decidedly amusing; she looked like
an angry hen.

"*What* is so funny?" she demanded. "What
you did is probably illegal."

"Yes, likely," he agreed politely. Thank
heaven for *wasta,* and the fact that he had plenty.
He rarely called in his royal title, but it's clout
had been very useful today, not that Tobi would
want to hear that story. "Water?"

"You can go to hell."

"Gladly, after I'm done with our business

this afternoon." His voice hardened. "Look at me, Tobi."

She glanced up. If looks could kill… He continued, his voice showing a calm he did not feel.

"The fact that you ignored me is completely unacceptable. What if it was an emergency?"

Her chin began to shake, and he could see her cheek dimple inward ever so slightly, as if she'd bit it to hold back tears. "I stayed out of your way," she said, staring down at the small glass table in front of her. "It's what you wanted, isn't it? It's what you *paid for."*

"So you didn't answer this to be petty," he pointed out. It was what he wanted, and he'd told her with no hesitation.

"My motives are none of your business."

She'd changed, he thought. She was just as beautiful as she'd ever been, but some of the spark he remembered had gone out of her eyes. He felt a sudden pang of remorse that surprised him; after all, he'd had his reasons for cutting her off thoroughly. He still remembered the hazy attraction of that night and how intense their kisses had been.

Pull yourself together.

"You'll come with me," he said briskly. "My jet is ready to go. I'll explain everything there."

She drew back. "I'm not going anywhere with you."

He laughed without humor. "You will, or I'll ban you from every country you attempt to enter, including your own. So, choose. Stay in transit hell—" he stood, smoothed his trousers "—or come with your husband and have a nice, *reasonable* chat aboard a private jet. Your choice, *my love*."

At that, Tobi's face hardened, and she stood. "You must be crazy to think I'll follow you anywhere. No, Akil. I'm not a child to be ordered round by you, and despite whatever you've conjured in that small mind of yours, you're not a despot or anyone with power. You've got my attention. Either speak your piece or get out."

Their eyes met as wills clashed for a moment; then Akil sighed before speaking the words he could barely believe himself were true.

"My brother, Malik, is dead."

Akil relayed the shocking events with as much feeling as if he'd been discussing the weather and for a moment, they didn't register because of that.

"Malik—" she echoed dumbly. She remembered Malik, of course—a taller, harder-edged version of her husband. He'd danced in a perfectly correct but expressionless matter at their wedding, and had kissed her cheek with lips so cold she'd winced a little. Still, he'd seemed rather healthy—

"Blood clot, they say. Completely undetectable and just as unavoidable," Akil said crisply. "Painless, I suppose that's a good thing. Two days ago."

"I—I hadn't heard." Why on earth did he look like that? She knew that Akil tended toward the stoic, but he looked positively unmoved.

"Djoboro is small, and no formal announcement has yet been made. Most people wouldn't be able to name the current ruler, for all their airs."

Tobi didn't know what to react to first—the news, which was horrific enough, or Akil's cold relaying of the news. "I'm so sorry, Akil," she said weakly.

He gave no other acknowledgment than a brief lift of his shoulders. "You see now," he said, "why I needed to reach you. I'm expected to return to Djoboro tomorrow."

"And?" Tobi's face must have still registered confusion because Akil was staring at her as if he couldn't quite believe she was being so thick.

"Malik has been acting as regent for two and a half years." Akil's voice finally showed some hints of strain. "I am his *brother,* Tobi, and the spare heir to the crown. Malik's wife, Jamila, had no children. And if indeed I am the regent king, that makes you—"

Tobi felt quite faint, and Akil's full mouth curved up into the first genuine smile of the afternoon, rusty as it was. "Sit," he said, almost kindly, and Tobi did, feeling she had to.

"I'm—"

"Yes. You are, as of two days ago, acting queen consort of Djoboro." He paused to let that sink in. "Perhaps we should have commenced with the divorce much earlier."

"It's hard to divorce someone you've convinced yourself doesn't exist," Tobi snapped, forgetting momentarily that he'd lost a brother and she should, at the moment, try to be comforting. Why, anyway, would she bother, when he clearly wasn't bothered himself? She raised her chin. "I'm very sorry for Malik's death, but again, I'm not sure why I'm here. I agreed to marry you so you could get your inheritance, and you've done very well with it. Otherwise, you made it more than clear you want nothing to do with me." Bitterness made her words sharp. "As far as I'm concerned, I've more than fulfilled my part of the bargain."

Akil's eyes glittered, and Tobi lifted her chin, crossing her arms across her chest. The past three years had wrought many changes in the young woman who had trembled in her husband's arms on their wedding night. She'd made her own way in the world, perhaps not as nobly as her stuck-up husband, but she'd done it. She'd made a name for herself, and she'd vowed many times along the way after that dreadful night with Akil that no man would ever make her feel less than worthy again.

That, and the fact that she was married, made for both a quiet and cold bed, but she'd learned to ignore it. She'd rather die a virgin if it kept her self-respect intact. Akil had the power to strip it from her with a few well-chosen words, but only if she let him.

She wasn't going to let him. Then he spoke, his voice casual and calm.

"I know you're angry." He moved in closer, eyes dark with something very much like—triumph, and this made her even angrier. He was so sure he had her. "It's quite a skill, being able to blow through that amount of money in only three years."

Tobi felt as if he'd struck her. "I—"

"I'd make it worth your while if you came back. No—no need to get up in arms, Tobi," he said at her outraged expression. "I have very little curiosity as to how much money you've handed to Hermès, or whomever—"

"I used that money to go to school!" cried Tobi, not even sure why she was defending herself; it was what they all thought of her, wasn't it? "And I made an investment that didn't—"

Akil waved a hand. "Again, not curious. I helped you then. Now I need a queen, and unfortunately for you, we are married. I don't see how you have a choice."

Tobi felt as if she'd been set on fire.

"If you think," she said icily, "that you can come here and bully me into acting as your queen, Akil Al-Hamri, you've another think coming. I'm not a child, and you haven't asked me a single thing—you've *demanded* it. You've made absolutely insulting assumptions about my doings, and you've shown up out of the blue after ghosting me for three years. You haven't even shown one iota of regret that your brother is dead!"

"My only regret," Akil gritted through his teeth, "is the fact that I have to go back."

Tobi made a noise of mock sympathy through her nose. "What a pity, the playboy prince who outwitted the evil royal family has to go back and do his duty. Finally act like a man, instead of a spoiled child—"

Akil visibly recoiled at that, and part of Tobi was horrified at the words speeding from her mouth without any hint of slowing down. It was as if all the hurt and resentments of the past few years had culminated in this single moment, and she was as intent on hurting him as he had her...

It probably shouldn't have hurt this much, she thought, suddenly tired. The problem had been that deep down inside, she'd wanted attention from him, hadn't she?

She could not say much more, however, for Akil turned on his heel and walked out of the lobby of the hotel.

CHAPTER FOUR

HAD HE SPOKEN, he would have cursed her. Not because of her harsh words—the headlines she'd clearly been reading about him over the past three years must have stuck quite firmly in her brain. No, it was her ill-timed accusation about Malik that made the blood throb in his temples!

Akil had never cared what people thought his reasons might be for exiting the royal family—they would think what they wanted anyway, and for months, North Africa had buzzed with rumors. The pet one—and the one that his wife clearly favored—was the one that painted him as a spoiled, entitled royal brat who wanted to spend his life partying on yachts and plowing through beautiful women while his father's health failed.

Now, with the weight of the invisible crown already on his head, how could he get Tobi to do what he wanted...needed? He mentally reviewed what he knew about the young woman—

fearless, headstrong, stubborn, nothing like her more docile older sister. *And considerably more attractive.* The odd thought appeared, unbidden, and he frowned, shook his head, returned to his train of thought.

His brother's death must have him more unsettled than he'd thought. Malik. He closed his eyes briefly. The last time he'd seen him was on the night of his wedding. Pain wanted to come and wash over him; he wanted to both cry out and clench his teeth against the unfairness of it all. Malik had been born to rule— he'd thrived on the hope of it since childhood. When their father's memory started fading over two years ago, shortly after Akil and Tobi's wedding, Malik had taken the regency gladly, though the event had been tinged with sorrow. He'd contacted Akil, asking him to come home. He hadn't. And he never would have, had this not happened. Now it wasn't just an individual imploring him to come home, it was an entire country. And care little as he might for his family, Akil cared a great deal for Djoboro. He loved his country with all his heart. Hell, Djoboro was the reason he'd stayed long after it was healthy anymore, long after he'd realized there was no role for him in his family except for that of troublemaker. He'd married, he'd left. He'd been the happiest he'd ever been for the past three years. However, his past had caught up with him in more ways than one. He had no brother. His father mentally was no more. And he had a wife, who by every indication wanted nothing to do with him.

What was wrong with her? Yes, there had been no communication between them since they'd gone their separate ways, but hadn't he provided for her financially, even more than their agreement had stipulated? He would be lying if he said he hadn't been curious, or if he said he'd never thought about the undeniable attraction that had led to the brief passion of their wedding night. It hadn't just been lust that night; it'd been a profound protectiveness that had scared the hell out of him. There was no way he would ever be able to make her happy; his upbringing had left him with no tools to do so. And that night, even beneath the haze of passion they'd found themselves in—

Tobi had kissed him that night like a woman who needed more than he had the capacity to give. There'd been no artifice there, nothing but an earnest wish to be closer to him. And that had scared the hell out of him. Using each other to escape was one thing—starting something as risky as a relationship with a woman he could hurt was another. He never, ever in his life wanted to give another human being even a fraction of the pain he'd grown up with, and the way she'd looked at him that night—

It scared the hell out of him.

So he'd cut her off as thoroughly as he had his family. His sole concentration had been on Ra Industries—and he had succeeded there, far beyond his wildest dreams. Somewhere, buried in his mind, had been a desire to share his success with Malik when he was ready, give Djoboro the opportunity to invest in *his* business.

Now he'd never have that chance.

Akil squeezed his eyes shut against another wave of distress; if he gave in to it, in to any of it, he'd never be able to do what needed to be done, which was to get his wife and go home. It would be easy enough to force her into doing what needed to be done; for all her bravado, Akil was very schooled in manipulation. After all, his family had been experts, and part of why he'd left. But there was something in the wide set of his wife's eyes and a tremble about her mouth that struck something very much like conscience in Akil's chest.

He didn't have the strength to fight dirty. Not tonight.

Akil took a moment to steady himself, then turned and walked back into the lobby. Tobi hadn't moved; she sat with her knees pressed together, suddenly looking very much like the young woman he'd taken to Dubai that night just a few years ago. She'd been just as beautiful then, and just as distressed, and he'd responded to her just as strongly. Memories came rushing back in bits and pieces, more suggestions than actual scenes. Soft, sweet lips and scented skin. A warm body pressed against his. An exhale of breath and a trembling frame. And not all those reactions had been hers, were he honest.

He'd kissed her in a moment of impulse, a moment of weakness that he refused to dwell on, and she'd responded so very readily. He took it as a mark of pride that he hadn't let things go further than they did. But now, looking at her face…

Akil pushed the thought from his mind. Enough thinking. He had to get Tobi to come back with him, and he realized he might know just how to do it.

The Djoboran royal jet hadn't changed at all since Tobi was last in it. Then, she was a new bride, shaky with adrenaline and having successfully escaped virtual captivity. Now she was a woman wedded but not wanted—until now.

She and Akil sat silent and hollow-eyed in the main cabin, pods swiveled to face each other. A flight attendant had served them tea with a flourish, then bowed deeply and retreated. It sat untouched between them, along with an array of gorgeous pastries, gleaming with honeyed pistachios in layers of thin dough and sprinkled with gold dust. Akil did not seem to want to speak; his eyes were focused on somewhere just above her left shoulder, and his spirit was far, far away. He'd asked her to come on board after he returned, saying that the quiet and privacy would be better than anything they could produce in the busy airport.

Tobi had agreed. After all, he'd lost his brother, and that was a fact she could not ignore. Now she endured the silence and picked at one of the sweets she'd been served before she couldn't take it anymore.

"Are you all right?" she said.

Akil's eyes flickered over her face, and his mouth twitched, just a little. "Truthfully, no. But I don't want to talk about it." His fingers idled at his own pastry. "I expect I should ask for your forgiveness."

"Don't, unless you mean it," Tobi replied, crossing her arms.

"No, I mean it," he said, and suddenly it was hard to breathe, because his eyes were fixed on her with an intensity that made her blood run hot. "I am sorry for ignoring you. I had my reasons."

"As I had mine for reaching out to you in the

first place," Tobi said quietly. "You think very little of me, don't you? Just like everyone else."

Akil winced visibly. "Fair comment. What happened?"

Tobi chewed her lip for a moment, trying to gauge his sincerity. "I think it matters little in the light of what's going on—"

"Earthly things matter little to Malik now," he said drily, "but you and I are still here. I appreciate your concern. Go on."

Not even a sign of traditional grief. She eyed him for a minute before speaking. "I—it was stupid. I had this idea to set up a safe house back home, for women who need help and have no other options. A safe place to go until they're back on their feet, or can fend for themselves, no matter where they're from. Medical care, financial assistance, business loans—"

"I get it." There was a gleam in Akil's eyes. "It's a very good idea."

"Yes, but it was executed quite badly. Investing in Nigeria is risky as it is because of the levels of corruption, and I didn't make the smartest contacts." She'd been colossally ripped off was more like it, but that part of the story was still too painful to explain in detail. "I lost everything. And so—I contacted you."

"Ah."

It was only one word, only the smallest bit of

acknowledgment, but the intensity in his eyes was enough to steal her breath away. The indifference was completely gone; for the first time, it felt as if he were looking at her, the real her. The Tobi who sometimes thought so little of herself, and strove so hard to do better.

Then he looked down, and the moment was dissolved.

"Malik and I were estranged at the time of his death," Akil said. His jaw was clenched hard, and there was a new glimmer in his eyes that hadn't been there before. Not tears—that would have been far too much for Akil—but some deep-seated, unspoken emotion. It grabbed Tobi round the throat like some dark force, pulled her in.

"I have to go back," he added, simply. "And I need your help if I'm to pull this off successfully. It isn't a ruse, not this time. I plan to stay."

She swallowed. "And me?"

"It's essential, for many reasons, that I have the woman I married by my side." All rage and arrogance was gone from his face now; he was sunken-eyed, an exhausted apparition that barely resembled the man who'd accosted her in the airport. "In return, I'll help you get your business back up and running. I will make sure it succeeds."

"More quid pro quo?" Tobi asked, a little more acidly than she first intended.

Akil raked his fingers through the thick hair on his head. "No, Tobilola, I'd do it even if you said no to this. It's a splendid idea," he continued. "And you clearly possess the heart of a queen, even though you don't want to take on the role."

Those words, simply spoken, broke something in Tobi that evaporated the anger like the morning mist, and she felt tears spring quick and hot to her eyes. Akil appeared to take no notice; he was turning a teacup over in his hand. It looked absurdly small in his long fingers.

"All right," she whispered. "I'll do it."

There was no triumph in Akil's face; he looked far too exhausted for that. He reached out and took her hand, ran his thumb over where her pulse beat wildly in her wrist; then he gently placed it back in her lap. "I'm going to give orders for the steward to get your things, and we'll be off as soon as we get clearance, if it's all right with you?"

She nodded, wiping furtively at her cheeks with her hands. "All right. And—I'm sorry about your brother."

"Kind of you to say," Akil replied. He stood and was gone in moments.

Now, hours later, and in flight, Tobi wondered if she'd made a mistake. After a deliciously hot savory meal served when they reached cruising altitude, Akil launched into the first of many speeches, all traces of what had been before completely gone.

"We land in a couple of hours," Akil said crisply once their plates had been cleared. "At the border of Djoboro and Morocco, there's a place there where the kings are buried, and Malik..."

"I understand," Tobi said quietly.

"There are protocols for the ceremony, of course, but—" And here, Akil drew a breath. "There will be a memorial back in Djoboro. Open to family and friends, and broadcast to the general public. It will need to be warm. Personable. Relatable."

"All right," Tobi said slowly.

"My sister-in-law, Jamila, will be on hand to answer any major questions, but she's understandably distraught. You'll be doing a lot of the heavy lifting."

It took a moment for this to register; then the tea cart was in danger again, for Tobi sat up straight. "Wait—what? You expect me to plan this?"

His brows lifted. "Not *plan*, exactly, but we need a member of the family to oversee the team that does it. You cannot possibly expect Jamila to subject herself to that kind of work when she's lost her husband so suddenly, and my father—" If his voice faltered a little on that word, he recovered quickly. "The man is mentally inept. I doubt he remembers what he ate for breakfast."

The casual cruelty of the statement stole her breath away. "He's your *father.*"

"So my mother told me."

"What is wrong with you?"

Akil's mouth twisted.

"And you won't have any input?"

He looked at her as if she were crazy. "Of course not."

"But he's your brother!"

"This isn't a line of conversation worth having," he said, and extended his legs. "Are you going to do it or not?"

Tobi gaped. "You don't want any involvement with this at all?"

"I have too much to do, Tobilola."

"But it's your brother! And I only met him once. You can't possibly expect me to—"

"Our team will have you apprised of everything from his education to his usual drink order, and there's thousands of hours of footage of him in our family archives. Give me something to do at the service, if you want, although I'd prefer to not do anything."

Tobi sagged back into her seat, and Akil

began to busy himself with post-dinner cocktails, muttering under his breath. "Never so glad to see wine in my life. You should have some more tea, though, Tobi. You look a little faint."

A dumbfounded Tobi allowed him to hand her a glass teacup of an amber brew that smelled deliciously of mint and spice. "Mind, it's hot."

Tobi didn't know how to address this. Running a memorial service as her first act as queen, and for a man who'd proven to be nothing but exacting—and frankly, far more complicated than she remembered?

She sipped.

The tea was sweet and bracing, and the spices seemed to permeate her senses, soothe her churning stomach. She focused on the fine carvings in the glass for as long as she could, and when she looked up Akil's eyes were on her face.

"I thank you for doing this," he said, and though the words were stiff they were not ungracious. "It makes it…easier."

"What happened was tragic," Tobi conceded, and nearly fell off her seat when Akil spoke again. This time his gaze was fixed on the window, on the rectangle of sky that glowed white-blue through the velvet curtains. He looked as if he wanted to take to the skies himself. Tobi knew in a way exactly how he felt; she'd often worn the same expression, flying home from brief diplomatic trips with her parents, short bursts of excitement in a monotonous life.

"…people like you," Akil was saying, startling her from her reverie.

"Excuse me?"

His gaze dropped down to her face, though she had the feeling he still wasn't seeing her, not really. A part of her wanted desperately to follow him wherever he was—somewhere inside there, he must be grieving. But when he spoke, his voice was still steady and impersonal.

"I've followed your…online presence. You're very personable, Tobi. Warm. Funny. People connect with you. My people connect with you." The words were staccato, brief, and said as if they were foreign on his tongue. "My popularity has not been…high since I left."

"You left to do a good thing," Tobi said, confused.

His lips curved into a smile that didn't reach his eyes. "Perhaps, but the press chose to concentrate on other things instead, and my father's PR machine worked overtime to ensure his people thought I wasn't—well. It's a long story."

"You're still the son of the house."

He made a noise under his breath. "You'll see. My return may be rather unpleasant. You, on the other hand, you've already got quite a following. Our wedding generated a great deal of public interest in Djoboro, and there are people who've followed you with fascination. Schoolgirls, naturally, might be the biggest group, with all the princess worship. Women. Families. I've been castigated for abandoning you. It's not an ideal way to begin my rule."

Oh—*why* was Akil this complicated? She'd never known a man who could enrage her, frustrate her, sadden her and drive her to sympathy within a few sentences. What was it her father always said? She licked her lips, trying to remember before she spoke.

"Ilé ọba tójó ẹwà ló bùsi," she said, and smiled a little at the look of confusion on her husband's face. "It means that the king's house burned, and he added beauty to it. You will turn this into something wonderful. You brought the sun to Morocco, after all, didn't you? You'll do better for Djoboro."

She did not know where the words came from, or the confidence with which she uttered them. And for a moment, she thought she'd reached Akil as well. A glimmer of what in a normal person might be hope brightened his eyes for a fraction of a second.

Then his face settled back into its usual jaded caution.

"See? That's why you'll do great with the memorial service," he added brusquely, and cleared his throat. "Come, we've much more to go over."

CHAPTER FIVE

AKIL FULLY EXPECTED an ice-cold reception upon arriving back in Djoboro, and the royal family more than adequately played their parts. He and Tobi landed at the border of Morocco, then were flown by helicopter over the Djoboran range, whose majesty was shrouded in desert twilight. Tobi was fatigued; he could see it in her eyes, though she didn't allow it to show in the set of her shoulders or the angle of her chin. Good. She would need that strength in the coming days. Aside from absolutely necessary courtesies, no one had approached the royal couple, offered any words of consolation. They were too grieved, and Akil fancied he saw a resentment in the dark eyes of the members of the court that they were loath to hide. It only made him set his shoulders higher, lift his chin.

Over the centuries, royal Djoborans were buried in the Valley of the Kings, a shallow dip at the base of the Djoboran range, shrouded from view of the main road by an obligingly craggy landscape. As a child Akil found the place terrifying. Now the site suited his mood perfectly. There were no palaces or fine houses here, only the imposing mausoleum, stretching as if trying to touch the sky, and a pillared, wall-less shelter to accommodate witnesses who were expected to leave that same day. There were never any visitors here, no offerings of fresh flowers or any sentimentalities. The former rulers of Djoboro were left to their own devices here, and now Malik was to join them.

Malik, who'd tried to reach out to him numerous times in the past few years, only to be rejected.

I'm not sorry for it, Akil told himself. He'd made that decision about his brother years ago, and if there was one thing Akil did not permit, it was regret. But standing here in the oppressive heat of the North African sun and listening to the final declarations made over his brother's coffin, he found himself clenching his jaw so hard against roiling emotion it hurt.

They'd been boys once, and best friends, before their differences and their father's attitude tore an irreparable rift between them. Perhaps he should not have blamed Malik? He'd been a child himself, after all; it wasn't his job to protect Akil.

The ceremony was bone-wearyingly long. There was a long recitation for both years of the young king's rule, detailing his accomplishments and his service to the crown. There was a tribute to his widow Jamila, who he knew must be buckling under the silent reproach of having not conceived an heir in their five years of marriage. Akil would have been a tolerable king had there been an end in sight to his rule; now, Djoboro was stuck with a regent king that nobody wanted or respected.

Why am I even here?

As if reacting to his inner turmoil, he felt Tobi stir at his side. In his ruminations, he'd literally forgotten she was there. She glanced up at him, face half shrouded by the heavy veils she wore, and he was startled when she slid a small hand over his, hesitating for the briefest of moments before closing it over his fingers.

She did not look at him again. And despite himself, Akil's heart began to beat a little faster. She felt sorry for him, and if Akil hated anything it was being pitied. But he also could not deny that his heart ached now with an intensity it never had before, and she was the only ally he had, reluctantly or not.

The king's house burned, and he added beauty to it.

He didn't drop her hand.

Thank heaven that's over, Tobi thought, closing her eyes and sitting back in the enormous tiled tub of her suite in the Djoboran royal coach.

Post-ceremony, the royal couple had been escorted to the decidedly old-fashioned form of transport, used for generations to ferry members of the royal family within the country. It would, Akil told her, take them directly to the capital, where Jamila's old apartments were being readied for their new occupant.

"Certainly we can't turn her out so soon," Tobi had protested. Jamila's pretty round face was drawn, and she had barely said a word to Tobi at the ceremony, but perhaps she shouldn't be expected to. "At the very least she should have her home. And I'm assuming the palace is large enough to—"

"You know how these things work, Tobilola," Akil had scoffed. "Royal life is not exactly about sentiment. The king dies, the new king takes his place. Period. And Jamila was hardly there. Malik only ruled for two years."

"Still," murmured Tobi.

"You're headed for failure if you plan on letting your emotions rule you. Excuse me, I have matters to attend to." Akil had stridden off with one of the many robed advisers that to Tobi had completely interchangeable faces. She was relegated to the care of a silent middle-aged woman who spoke no English; she took Tobi through swaying, drafty corridors to a comfortable suite that consisted of a sleeping car, a lounge and a bathing car.

"Mamlaka?" she asked, a little hesitantly, not sure if she was using the sovereign title correctly.

The woman understood. She pointed to a small door on the north end of the sleeping car, one that presumably led to Akil's suite. She then briskly drew an enormous tub of steaming water, produced a number of fragrant bottles that were sprinkled in and stood imperiously, pointing to Tobi's sandals, dress, veil and overdress until she shed them.

Tobi had done traditional hammams while on vacation, of course, and this bath seemed to be a condensed version. Her attendant scrubbed her vigorously first with soap and soft flannel and then with a preparation that felt a bit grittier than sand-crushed seashells, perhaps, in fragrant paste. Then came oil, rubbed into every crevice, and scraped off with a curved, sickle-shaped tool. The woman was too matter-of-fact for Tobi to be embarrassed, and in moments

Tobi was settled in pleasantly hot water that reached her chin, made her skin tingle.

The woman said something to her, patted her on the cheek almost maternally, and was gone, leaving Tobi alone with her thoughts. She closed her eyes, leaned her head back, tried a little idly to identify what the pillow beneath her head was stuffed with. Pine needles? Eucalyptus? Whatever the delicious blend, it was loosening the bands of anxiety and tightness at her temples.

When the door of the car rattled open, she didn't even open her eyes. Doing so might risk how absolutely comfortable she was. "I wish I knew how to ask for a top-up of hot water," she murmured.

"There's a tap for your foot on the lip of the tub," a deep voice said, and Tobi shot upward so violently that a wave of water threatened to cascade over the edge.

"I—what are you—"

"You summoned me?"

"Summoned for where?" Tobi threw an arm over her chest. This sort of bath didn't even have the benefit of bubbles to hide beneath, and her body felt as if it'd been set ablaze. She twisted and looked over her shoulder to see Akil regarding her with decided amusement.

"Turn around!" she shrieked.

"So you didn't call for me?" He did turn, but

not before a smirk and a languid skim of the length of her that made her face heat more than the bath.

"I certainly did not!" Her mind raced, and then she groaned, standing up and wrapping the towel round her body. The train was swaying gently now, and she had to clutch the fine brass handrails with all her might before climbing out; the tiles were slippery with oil. In her scramble to get out fast, her feet went out from under her. Akil whirled around in a flash and caught her upper arms.

"No, don't!" she cried, scrambling for the rectangle of luxurious Egyptian cotton that hid her modesty.

"Don't be ridiculous," Akil said roughly. He was at her side, supporting her to sit up. He removed the heavy brocaded dressing gown he was wearing and draped it over her shoulders. It smelled so like him that Tobi felt quite dizzy for a moment. She clutched the fabric around her damp body, and only when it was secure did she turn her head.

"Are you all right?"

"Fine," she mumbled, more embarrassed at her overreaction than the fall itself. Akil now wore nothing except a pair of white cotton trousers, tied carelessly with a frayed drawstring, and considerably dampened by the water from her bath…

She drew her gaze upward in near panic. She'd never seen Akil in any state of undress before, and the lean hardness of his body was simply too much. He was hairless, and had obviously had a bath of his own; his brown skin gleamed in the soft light as if touched by bronze. Shadows placed every muscle in sharp relief, and his face, softened by amusement, was a fitting crown for it.

She squeezed her eyes shut. Maybe if she wished hard enough she'd find him gone when she opened them.

"Your hands are shaking," Akil said, and the gentleness in his voice made a lump form in her throat. Perhaps she was more tired than she thought. "Come on, Tobi. Up, and let's go. Your lounge car will be much warmer. We might be in the desert, but the nights are very cold."

Tobi opened her eyes and wordlessly took Akil's extended hand.

"You're not talking," he pointed out, and tugged her forward.

"I'm embarrassed," she said through gritted teeth. "I don't know why. I did ask after you, but I have no idea why Hajar would tell you I wanted you!"

"She likely assumed you wished me to catch

you in the bath. You did look very fetching," Akil drawled, and the blaze of head-to-toe heat was back.

"I would *never,* even if we were actually—" She swallowed. "We buried your brother today!"

Akil lifted his bare shoulders. They'd reached the sliding door between the cars in her suite, and he shoved them open with perhaps a little more force than was necessary. "All the more reason to comfort your grieving husband, no? It went well. I'm sure you're exhausted."

Akil guided her through the lounge, seemingly unconcerned by his near nakedness. She couldn't take her eyes off the hollow at the base of his back, or the tensing of muscles beneath his skin as he walked. What was wrong with her, ogling him as if—

"Sit down. I'll ring for tea and something to eat," Akil ordered, settling her on a velvet-covered chaise longue.

"Please, some cool water as well," Tobi murmured, squeezing her thighs together as tight as she could. She knew it was exhaustion and nervousness, but she was suddenly terrified she'd cry. Beneath the heavy layer of brocade, her body was beginning to do things utterly outside her permission. It fairly hummed with an odd energy that she knew had very much to do with Akil. Her skin was tingling, and she'd never felt more aware of how heavy her breasts hung beneath the layer of embroidered fabric. It rubbed against nipples that were growing harder and more sensitive by the moment, and she crossed her arms, trying to still their movement. No hopes there. She'd stopped growing taller soon after primary school, much to her annoyance, but her breasts and hips had had a mind of their own and kept going long afterward.

Usually, she considered that an asset. Not today, though. And Akil seemed totally oblivious. When he came close to her, filling her space with that delicious scent, those trousers riding low on his hips… She dropped her eyes and skittered back a bit. She felt incredibly foolish, but she couldn't have stopped herself any more than she could stop breathing.

"What?" he demanded.

"I—just—could you—please put something on?"

Surprise lit his eyes, followed by that vague amusement she never was sure was real or not. "You're wearing my dressing gown," he pointed out.

"Please," she said, and he laughed for the first time since they'd reconnected in Dubai. He left, and in moments returned, tugging a white djellaba down over his stomach. The robe was

stiff with newness and nearly touched the floor round his feet.

"Better?" he said a little arrogantly, and settled himself next to her.

"Thank you," Tobi said, and stared down at her hands. She wished it were better. He was covered now, yes—but his half-naked form had been firmly imprinted in her brain, and she knew it wasn't going anywhere anytime soon.

CHAPTER SIX

So the party princess, the socialite of the year, was easily embarrassed by the sight of a half-naked man. *Interesting.*

Tobi hadn't looked at his face since he'd re-entered the room, and was guzzling ice water as if she'd just run a marathon. She looked quite fetching in his dressing gown, he had to admit. The brocaded fabric swathed her curves tightly—and what magnificent curves they'd been, soft and supple with water and oil. Oh, yes—he'd seen everything, and the reality was just as enticing as her form-fitting wardrobe had promised.

He'd married a beautiful woman, in body as well as face. And a denser person than either of them would be able to discern the tension in the room. It was no surprise for him; Tobi was very attractive, after all. Any man would be stirred at the sight of her. But her reaction to *him*—

It was a distraction, and a welcome one. It

chased out the darkness of the thoughts that had been crowding his head since he'd received the news of his brother's death. It reduced everything to the here and now—the two of them, the seclusion, the soft lighting, the fact that he knew precisely how naked she was beneath his robe. His wife, to take if he wanted, to release some of the tension that had held his body taut for days. It would chase out the memories and the threat of the mental regression to the hurt, angry young man he'd been.

You need this. And from the way Tobi's chest rose and fell, he did not think he'd be unsuccessful if he tried. Her lashes were fluttering rapidly over smooth cheeks; he suddenly was reminded of another night, three years ago, and he knew that in some ways this was a continuation of what he'd left unfinished then.

There were many words of seduction that he knew he could use on Tobi that night, but the memory of their wedding night stole them from him. Instead he extended his hands in silent invitation.

Tobi pressed her fingers to her cheeks. "It's— Akil, I don't know."

"Just allow me to hold you for a moment, *habibti,*" he said smoothly, and then she was there in his arms, pressed full against his chest. It was odd, in a sense, for tenderness was blunting the edges of the lust he expected to feel, and his hands did not go to her body, but to her face.

This was an entirely different type of distraction than he'd intended.

"The coach is beautiful," she said.

"I suppose it's decorated in better taste than the airplane," he conceded. "This is just the beginning. My people love luxury."

She was looking up at him curiously, and her expression was troubled. "I don't understand you," she blurted out. "We buried your older brother today, your father is ill, and you will be made king in a few days. King of an entire country you didn't even want, and you're not speaking about any of it."

"There are much more pleasant topics at hand," he said, a little more sharply than he intended. He trailed his fingers down to the hollow in her neck where rubies and gold had rested on their wedding day; funny, he could remember exactly how she looked. "I'm thinking about our wedding night, for example, and how lovely you looked."

She licked her lips. "You're trying to distract me."

"Indeed I am," he agreed.

"Are we never going to discuss—"

"No, because there is nothing *to* discuss." He managed to temper his voice a little more this time. "All I'm interested in at the moment is you, Tobilola, and how lovely you look in this light."

"Surely you don't think I can be waylaid by—" she said a bit breathlessly.

"I'd like to try."

He dropped his mouth to her neck, kissing the tender skin there, and Tobi actually whimpered. "Akil, this isn't—"

"Would you feel better about this if I admitted I was heartbroken? If I said I loved my brother dearly and will miss him for the rest of my life?" Tobi flinched at his sarcasm, but her soft breaths were coming faster at the sound of his voice, and at the brush of his lips that followed every sentence. He was moving upward now, toward his real target; the full, soft mouth that was parted with want, despite herself. He'd never touched a woman whose body was so delightfully reactive. "I'm not a liar, Tobi."

"But—"

"You know nothing about my family, or me." And it was true. He'd married Tobi as part of a deal, and there was no way she would be the one to draw out what he'd kept hidden for years, even though his body now felt more alive than it had been in months. "If you want me to stop, now is the time to say it," he said, his voice husky.

"You're not yourself," she said a little help-lessly, and he laughed against the soft fold of skin at the corner of her mouth.

"I assure you that I've never felt more like myself than I do today." Then, as if falling upon some delicacy he'd been saving for hours to enjoy at his leisure, he kissed her.

Yes. This was exactly what he needed.

After a moment of frozen hesitation, Tobi matched his urgency so intensely it startled him. She kissed him hungrily, as if she'd wanted this forever. Her mouth tasted of honey, spice, car-damom and something vaguely familiar, an es-sence that hung round her that had stayed with him since that first night. Unfinished business, yes, that's what this was, and their bodies re-membered exactly where they'd left off, even if their mouths refused to admit it. And if he managed to do this, managed to get her to a place where nothing mattered but the slide of skin on skin, he might also be able to banish all the ghosts that threatened to disturb his peace tonight.

He was using her. And she was letting him, frankly.

She should be angry, ashamed, horrified! She should be anything but what she was now, softening even more beneath his touch, arching her body up to him in clear invitation.

They were picking up where they'd left off, in a sense, and she wanted it badly.

Tobi shifted, her fingers catching his biceps, her leg sliding between his, and he grunted, slid his hands down for a greedy exploration of her bottom, her hips, palming both through the fabric she was draped in.

Tobi let out a sound that was half whimper, half moan, and in answer his hand curved round where one of her breasts rose soft and full beneath embroidered brocade. He thumbed her nipple through the fabric almost roughly; at this point they were so swollen, so sensitized, it was as if all the sensation in her body was reduced to those aching tips and a steady throb between her legs. He caught one between two of his fingers and tugged.

An oath escaped from her throat, and Akil chuckled. His hands were everywhere: her cheeks, her waist, her breasts. They found the braided belt on the dressing gown, the one she'd tied so securely, and toyed with it almost playfully.

"Akil—"

"Slowly," he said softly, and then he was drawing fabric from her shoulders, baring her breasts to his gaze.

He was so still for a moment she opened her eyes, and the look on his face brought that blaze of heat back, not embarrassed this time, but something far more primal. Whatever her reservations, all which seemed to have flown into the night, the mutual desire was undeniable. The swaying of the train was making her breasts move in a way that would have embarrassed her, but Akil's bold seduction had given her a wantonness that made her lift her chin instead, answering his look with a steady gaze of her own.

His mouth twisted a little, and then all her bravado was gone, for he tugged her close, palmed the heavy weight of her breasts in his hands. He was silent as he caressed her, first with gentle strokes of his fingers, then soft kisses, leaving her nipples untouched till they ached so badly she was virtually thrusting them at his mouth.

You know what I want. Stop teasing me. The teasing was not born of malice, though; it was a wish to draw out her pleasure to the highest point, until it was almost unbearable.

"Akil," she managed, and skittered violently as his thumb finally passed over her left nipple, circling the tight swollen bud slowly. Akil did not speak; instead he lowered his head to her other breast, catching her nipple between his teeth for *just* long enough and then sucking hard. For several moments the only sounds in the room were the few gasps she simply could not hold back and the hum and clack of the coach, hurtling toward its destination.

She might reach the peak of her pleasure just like this, she thought helplessly; her body had never been so tightly wound, so ready for it in her life. Akil's skillful fingers had left her breasts to slip through where the gown covered her thighs, and he was cupping her there now, the slickness she knew would be there surely on his skin. There was the barest brush, and she was gasping as her body tightened, then released, splitting into what felt like fragments of herself.

It'd taken so little.

Akil rocked her forward, and she buried her face in the crook of his neck. They were both breathing hard. She could feel the hardness of his arousal against her bare thigh, through the layers of clothing he still wore; she shifted against him, and he made a sound deep in his throat.

"Will you let me—" she began, then stopped. Akil shook his head.

"Not tonight," he said gently. "We will, but not tonight. I need all my wits about me tomorrow, and you need to sleep." He tipped her chin up, peered into her face. His eyes were dark as the night speeding past through the red-and-gold velvet curtains. "Tobi—"

A draft came over her bare skin, and she shivered. She made as if to draw the robe closed, and he helped her after the slightest hesitation.

"You are so very beautiful," he said simply, running his hands down the slender length of her, then pulling the material together over her breasts. "There is no reason this time together can't be—pleasant for both of us, Tobi."

Tobi felt her insides chill, and she shifted to full sitting position, ignoring the now-uncomfortable dampness between her thighs. "What are you saying? You wish me to act as your queen in all senses, even though you don't—"

She couldn't finish her sentence. To think of love would be nothing more than absurd. She couldn't even fathom why the word had come to her mind, except she knew in a helpless sort of way that if she let him, Akil could easily work his way into her heart. His gentle words to her about her suitability for queenship had eased open the gates.

"I am grateful for the service you're rendering," Akil said, and that full mouth of his curved up. "We've a lot in common, Tobilola. We left our situations, made something of ourselves. Although duty brings me back, you're under no such obligation, at least not forever." He paused and took a breath. "Plan what you're going to do later, Tobi. I have no intention of bringing you into the hell a rule can be. There is no place for you here. I won't allow it. Enjoy Djoboro, help me conquer public opinion—share my bed, if you desire. But know that you're free at the end of it."

His voice lowered on that last bit, and Tobi felt her insides cramp with unfulfilled want against the aching emptiness that hadn't been filled by him. There was another emptiness there, too, and this one was somewhere deep in the caverns of her heart. She'd married Akil to escape her father's oppression, but she hadn't yet found a home, had she? She'd had noble aspirations. She'd gone to school. She'd failed miserably at her first attempt at business. Since then it'd been a series of hotels, apartments and visits to fellow socialites, parties and schmoozing with the most ridiculous company. Now, looking at her husband, the king, she felt her failures more keenly than she ever had before.

In reality, she wanted to help people and have a place to call her own. And like an idiot, she'd let that want lead her into the kingdom and the arms of a man who would not offer her that, even if he could.

At least he was being honest.

She drew her knees up. Akil was no longer looking at her; he was staring out the window, as if in a trance, initiated by the steady click-clacking of the train. The heat between them had fully dissolved. She waited a full moment before she spoke.

"So what am I to do afterward, then?"

Either he did not note the catch in her voice, or he chose not to recognize it.

"You have plenty of time to figure that out," he said in a voice that she supposed was meant to be comforting, and eased to his feet. He hesitated for a moment, then bent and kissed her cheek. His own was like sandpaper against her soft skin.

"Get some rest, Tobilola," he said, not unkindly. "We arrive at the capital at dawn."

CHAPTER SEVEN

THE AFRICAN PRINCIPALITY of Djoboro, named for its ancient ties to Mali, hugged the coast of Morocco. It was small, exquisite, and it was her new home—for the time being, anyway. Hajar woke her with the dawn, opening the curtains of the royal coach wide, humming low to herself as she laid out toiletries and items to refresh her mouth, hair and skin that filled her chambers with a rich scent.

With the aid of a translator app on Tobi's phone, she explained they would pull into the capital in less than two hours. Akil was awake and with his advisers, and she was asked to kindly join him as soon as she was ready.

Tobi thoroughly enjoyed a solitary breakfast of eggs, fruit and creamy, sour *labneh* with cheese and fresh-baked bread, looking out to the soft oranges and purples of the early morning. In a way, she was glad that Akil didn't appear; after all the emotion of last night, he'd have ruined the serenity of the morning. She was treated to a hazy sun rendered in brilliant reds and oranges, rising over the red-brown hue of Djoboran mountains, all flanked by desert that seemed to stretch to infinity. In front of them she could make out the gray outlines of the sea, so far away it seemed to blend into the sky. When she finished eating, Hajar bustled her over to where her clothing was set out on the bed.

There was nothing there from her own wardrobe; it was all brand-new and exquisitely tailored, down to undergarments of some slippery, gauzy fabric so soft it felt like she wore nothing at all. The dress itself was a simple slip of corded cream silk that touched the ground round her feet, followed by a gauzy overdress embroidered heavily at the neck, hem and wrists with fine gold thread. She'd never seen such careful finishing; there wasn't a loose thread to be seen. There were beaded sandals and a matching belt; Hajar pulled and prodded until it encircled Tobi's slim waist to her satisfaction. Then, face pleased, she retreated from the room.

Only a few moments went by before there was a knock and the door slid open.

"Oh, good. You're ready. Almost."

It took Tobi a few moments to place the petite woman standing in the doorway. She was dressed similarly to Tobi, except her gown and overdress were of the deepest obsidian black. She carried a small mahogany chest in one hand, and a long black ribbon draped over the other.

"National dress suits you, I think," she said briskly. "There was a time when I would have killed for your height; long skirts absolutely swallow me up. Do you like it?"

"Very much." Tobi felt more than a little awkward. She hadn't seen Jamila since the funeral; she hadn't even known she was on the train! Akil hadn't deigned to give her that information the night before. "I—how are you doing?" she asked, reaching out an impulsive hand. She could still remember the death of one of the royal princes in her own father's house years before, and the devastated mood that had taken over the entire palace for days.

Jamila did not look displeased by her gesture, but she did look surprised. "Heavens, how good of you to ask, I'm fine. I'm here to help you prep for this morning. There will be a processional, and now that I am relegated by my husband's death to princess royal—" she said this with no apparent distress "—you must learn all my protocols."

Tobi kept from gaping, barely. What a family! Jamila's unlined face was perfectly serene; she didn't look distressed at all. In her smooth accented English she detailed the processional that would begin in an open car, followed by a walk across the country square, to the main palace.

"Then they'll ceremony you to death, with nary a cup of tea in sight," she wrapped up drily. "Your attendant will have water and cinnamon candy, so do signal for either if you ever feel faint. Keep your chin up, and never look directly at any camera, or some idiot blogger will accuse you of seeking them out. Pleasant half smile at all times, and one half pace behind the king."

Tobi nodded, wondering if she should be taking notes. "Where is he?" she asked falteringly, then immediately felt like an idiot for doing so.

"He'll be along shortly before we disembark. Sit down."

Tobi did promptly, and Jamila summoned Hajar, who brought in glasses of tea and a formidable- looking glass box of makeup brushes. As she worked on Tobi's face, Jamila drilled her charge.

"I know you've been married for three years. Have you learned Djoboran at all?"

"A few greetings," Tobi said hesitantly. *How could I when we weren't even together?*

"Say them."

Tobi did so, feeling rather foolish. Jamila nodded and corrected her pronunciation. "Your accent is rather pretty, though. Use them—it will be well spoken of. Any French? Arabic?"

"Only schoolgirl French, and I assure you that no one wants to hear that."

"We'll have to get you a tutor, then." Jamila sighed and drained the cup of Moroccan tea. "Yet another thing for us to do."

What kind of thing was this, expecting a widow of only a few days' time to shadow her? "Jamila, I'm sure you're preoccupied with much. I would hate to impose—"

"Impose on what?" her sister-in-law snorted. "I'm childless, I've lost most of my appointments, and I need to prove myself useful in something. This isn't an imposition, dear, it's duty. And duty isn't your husband's strong suit, so as usual, we women need to compensate."

"I think that Akil has very much proven his dedication to the crown," Tobi replied. "After all, he—"

"Don't talk, you'll spoil Hajar's work. And of course he hasn't." Jamila was maddeningly calm. "He's treating us all as if he's doing us a favor, and hasn't yet said a word to his poor father—"

You're wrong, Tobi wanted to retort. But she couldn't; what evidence did she have? After all, Akil himself had warned her about his own lack of popularity.

"I feel quite sorry for you, actually," Jamila finished. Hajar stepped back, finally pleased with her work, and Jamila wrapped a length of black satin ribbon round her sleeve.

"Mourning band," she informed her. *"I* will have to look like a crow for the next year, but the throne is above things as commonplace as human emotion. Full black on you and Akil is considered unseemly. Oh, there are dozens of rules. But you're starting with the advantage of not having a poor reputation, Tobi. Use it well, and your husband will give you whatever you want."

Jamila smiled, just a little, running her fingers through the locks of glossy hair not covered by her black mourning veil.

"Now you look like one of us," she said, her voice tinged with satisfaction.

Tobi looked and was quite startled at her reflection. Hajar had done wonders with all her pots and brushes; somehow Tobi's skin looked brighter, clearer. The *kajal* round her eyes and the false lashes she added made them look twice as large, liquid-dark against a clear background of white; her lips were full and touched with a gloss of berry-brown. She looked exactly like herself, only a greatly enhanced version.

"You really should wear no color other than white," Jamila remarked as if she were the author of her sister-in-law's beauty herself. "It brings out all the tints in your skin. No question why Akil married *you,* even though he had to go all the way to Nigeria to do it. Nothing to your older sister, of course, she was born with style, but you'll do. Now come, let me help you with this headdress, and coach you in the management of that skirt. The last thing we need is the new queen tumbling down during her first appearance."

The closer they got to the capital, the more stony-faced Akil became, and Tobi had no idea what to do about it. After her drilling by Jamila, she was led to the car used by the royal couple for entering and disembarking. It was outfitted simply with a thick silk rug so plush it muffled all sound and fat velvet-upholstered seating that ran round three out of four walls of the car. It was empty except for Akil, who had earbuds in, with a look of intense concentration on his face.

"I expect that Jamila has informed you of everything?" he said, glancing her way.

Tobi felt an odd thrill at the sound of his voice; her body immediately chose to associate it with other things, the husky way it'd sounded only the night before, saying all manner of things while his hands teased her breasts. She forced herself back to the present with some effort. Whatever Akil was thinking of, it clearly wasn't close to that: he was staring at her as blankly as if she'd been... Jamila.

"I'm ready," Tobi assured him. "But—Akil, I thought it—I mean, she's just lost her husband. I don't want to burden her with—"

Akil shook his head. "Burden her? It is her responsibility as monarch to share her knowledge. You don't shirk your responsibilities just because someone died, do you? What if you'd been her daughter?"

But what about time to grieve? Tobi thought. No one in the house of Al-Hamri seemed to have ever heard of the word; their hyper-focus on their rule was the only thing she'd seen spark any real emotion. Jamila was just as haughty as Akil was being now, and she'd seen no evidence that Malik had been any different. And the closer they moved to their destination, the stiffer, less animated her husband became. His face had darkened, become stormy. There was absolutely no hint of the humor, however slight, that had softened his mouth the night before. She cleared her throat. "I like the national dress," she said for the sake of saying something to lighten that awful silence. She smoothed her beringed hands over the embroidery.

"Good, because you'll be wearing a hell of a lot of it in the days to come," Akil said grimly.

"Jamila brought me some choice pieces from the vault," she continued, reaching up to touch the enormous rubied jewels dangling from her ears. They were fastened with a hook of gold that slid behind each ear; they were far too heavy, Jamila explained, to be worn the normal way.

Akil's responses became limited to grunts deep in his chest.

"Are you nervous?" she asked.

He shot her a contemptuous look. "No."

Well, excuse me. She wanted to ask if the old king was somewhere on this coach as well, if he was to make an appearance. No one had really referred to him at all in the time she'd been here, and she was curious; where was he? Surely he wasn't so ill that he needed to be hidden away?

She could recall the stern-faced man with deep grooves in his forehead and round his mouth. He and her father thoroughly enjoyed each other's company, and there was always a handful of sweets in his pocket for the children in the house whenever he visited.

"Will your father be there?" she asked after a moment.

Akil's face tightened even more; goodness, she hadn't thought it possible. "His presence is as irrelevant to this ceremony as his existence is to the crown."

Tobi gasped at the harshness of his words. "Akil—"

"It's true."

"But he's the former king!" Tobi protested. This cold, almost dismissive treatment, was it because he was ill? "Surely he can watch from somewhere quiet? He was well-loved, was he not? The people will want to see him."

"He may in his private apartments. I don't know his setup." Akil lifted and lowered his shoulders. "And if you are quite finished, Tobilola, I'd like to keep listening to this." He pointed to his earbuds.

Tobi was horrified, a horror that pushed away her anger at being so summarily dismissed. That poor old man! Inwardly she vowed that she would visit him as soon as she could, ensure that he was being treated well, at the very least, and maybe get some answers as to why Akil was being so cold.

CHAPTER EIGHT

THE ONLY GOOD thing about the processional, Akil thought grimly, was that Tobi had no idea what was going on.

He'd expected some degree of coolness from a crowd that had been coached for years to think him the worst sort of cad, but the people that lined the streets of Djoboro's main city square to watch the arrival of the new king greeted him with near silence. Not a reverent silence, but the type of silence produced by a group that is too polite to jeer. He knew he'd only escaped that because of Jamila; the small erect figure in her fluttering black robes drew roars of appreciation, as well as piles of the vivid star-shaped flowers that were the only real things of beauty agriculturists managed to coax from Djoboro's desert soil.

Tobi was greeted with a garland of them by three wide-eyed schoolgirls who giggled when she bent to greet them hesitantly, the words in traditional Djoboran awkward on her tongue. She followed up with some of the phrases she'd mastered on the way over, and the girls answered, clearly delighted that this new princess could speak to them, awkwardly as she managed. She spoke in soft, dulcet tones to everyone she met, personalizing the conversation for each of them: courtiers, the prime minister, representatives from other royal families.

The crowds were curious with Tobi, as well they might be; there was much craning of necks, enthusiastic applause and murmured conversation when she passed. Teenage girls seemed most excited to see her. Tobi stopped once, twice, three, four times to crouch and pose for cell phones held aloft. The new king received the customary bows of the head, but not a single person on that busy avenue made eye contact with him.

It stung Akil more than he'd ever admit.

After the processional came an extensive tour for Tobi's benefit, bolstered by a fat guidebook. Churches, mosques, casinos, historic sites and national parks all blurred together in a two-hour tour of the capital city. Akil made up for the churning low in his stomach by interrupting her official guide, adding a comment here, an anecdote there; he recalled official visits and events with encyclopedic accuracy. It was unnerving how much came back to him and how quickly, and the odd ache he felt at the sight of his old home.

Perhaps he'd missed it more than he thought. He knew his issues stemmed from the family he'd clashed with, not the land itself. And now, he was to enter the enormous palace of Djoboro as ruling monarch. An unpopular one at the moment, yes, and one who'd been self-exiled until a few days ago, but he was king. King!

At the end of the processional, the little band was placed inside a large black car and driven the last couple of miles to the palace. Akil had traveled this route many times before in many other processionals; he could clearly remember sitting in the back of the black limousines that were in style at the time, looking at his brother and his father. The two always sat side by side, knees brushing, talking in low tones about matters of state, future plans. Akil was not expected to participate, and was regarded by his father with astonishment when he did try...

It'll take you years to catch up, boy. Don't bother trying.

Now those words were haunting him. Since Malik's death there had been parliamentary letters. Thousands of notes from meetings he hadn't known existed. Recordings. Conversations with heads of state. Not to mention the

constant stream of updates from the conde-
scending advisers he'd inherited from Malik
and from his father, advisers who resented taking orders from the resident ne'er-do-well.

He wished he could fire them all, start anew.
But such would be impossible in Djoboro. They
were divinely appointed, products of a long line
of tradition. Even his ancestors seemed to want
to set him up to fail.

Why am I even doing this? He'd asked himself this question every single day. He'd barely
slept since Malik's death; there was simply no
time. If he was to conduct himself with any
modicum of competence at all, he had to plan
his day down to the millisecond. His advisers,
though helpful, lacked the sympathy that would
truly make their contribution meaningful.

And it was as if his brother hovered over his
shoulder, along with the man his father had
been, sneering at him. Willing him to fail. It
made his breathing shallow at the oddest times,
made him break into a cold sweat when he did
manage to sleep.

He told no one of this. Ghosts weren't real;
weakness was. And he had to crush this weakness beneath the heavy boot of achievement.

A curse on all of them, he thought, his jaw
tightening. Soon as he found his feet, he'd re-
place them all. And he'd move his wife and

himself to the private residence he'd used years ago; it was only a twenty-minute ride from the main palace.

There was no way he could pull this off under the accusing eyes of the past, and all the kings that had walked the corridors before him.

After the processional, and a banquet to welcome the royal couple that lasted till midnight, Tobi was shown to lush quarters that barely registered, given the hour. Then she was up at six again; that morning was her first official meeting of court, where she was formally introduced as Akil's wife to the members of the royal family. There were four besides Akil's: the Houses of Malik, Akram, Zaki, Yousef. Faces blurred, but she kept her back straight, kept that pleasant half smile fixed on her face.

Despite the long journey, Akil seemed to only grow stronger as the hours passed, with a freakish gleam in his eyes that worried her; she'd seen it in her father in years past, when the older man was working on a project and refused to take a break. He'd crack if he wasn't careful. For now, her husband seemed to sustain his energy with a steady stream of golden-brown Arabic coffee, candied pistachios and an ice-cold energy drink. His composure only seemed to waver in one meeting: a PR team had been flown in from the UK, specifically tasked with the new king's reputation and public perception. Here she learned precisely why Akil had needed her so badly.

"You're the lowest-rated monarch, by public poll," the leader of the team said bluntly. "Issues we've identified include leaving your position as a working royal three years ago—"

"I'm here now, am I not?" Akil said coldly.

"—abandoning your young wife, who is quite popular across the entire female demographic—"

Tobi felt herself flush, sat up a little straighter.

"—and most importantly, your relationship with the former king. There are rumors of a rift—"

"Not rumors. All true."

"Whether it is or not, it needs to be repaired in the public eye." The consultant's eyes were as calm as Akil's were stormy. "In short, Your Majesty, the public has been led to believe you're inconsiderate at best, mulish at worst, with no regard for tradition."

Akil's dark eyes had taken on a glitter she recognized. "Traditions change."

The man cleared his throat. "A public reconciliation—"

"Not going to happen," Akil said, and rudely. That meeting ended abruptly. And after several more Tobi found it hard to keep her eyes open. She would not ask Akil when she could take a rest, she was determined, but after six hours on the house floor with the scantest of water breaks, she stretched her eyes so wide open they burned. She blinked and reopened them one, two, three times, and—

"Wake up," her husband said, prodding her.

She flushed so hard beneath her skin she had to remove the linen jacket that Jamila had bullied her into wearing that morning, fanning herself with her notes. No one seemed to have taken notice.

Finally, blessedly, it was over, and she and Akil were in the back of yet another dark car, cinnamon-and-orange-scented air-conditioning wafting over them. She closed her eyes, too tired to even stress over the awkwardness of being alone with him, and in such close proximity. It felt like barely a second before Akil spoke into her ear.

"Tobi, we're here."

She blinked. They were in the driveway of an enormous stone-gray villa; she could not see much of it, as the compound was dark.

"This isn't the palace," she said, and a yawn nearly cracked her jaw into two. She opened her mouth to apologize for falling asleep again, but the words died on her lips when he smiled. The driver came round and opened the door for her; they eased out into the driveway and stood facing the house.

"You must be exhausted," he said, and his voice was the gentlest she'd ever heard it. Something inside her constricted at his tone. She would not admit it, but she was hungry for that kindness, and she hated herself a little for it. She could not afford to want this from Akil, she reminded herself, and lifted her chin.

"I can't believe you're not," she murmured. She opened her mouth to say something else, but another of the jaw-splitting yawns she'd been stifling for two hours appeared, and Akil chuckled.

"Like you Nigerians say, 'you really tired.' Let's go."

"I'm not sure I can even walk," she groaned, then yelped as Akil took a step forward, scooped her up into his arms with one seamless motion.

"Akil!" She looked round, scandalized. "You can't—"

"Don't you realize how romantic this makes me look?" he teased. "Hold still. I'm not as coordinated as I look."

That was an unlikely claim. She'd never felt as light as she did now, borne so easily in her husband's arms. His muscles were tensed and felt so incredibly solid that she relaxed into him despite herself, resting her head on his chest. His heart was thudding; the beat was steady, strong.

"Eyes are everywhere on Djoboro," he said into her ear. "And believe it or not, there was already a story this morning about our sleeping in separate rooms—as if my parents ever stayed together! Queens and kings never do."

Oh. She fought back her disappointment, then chastised herself for being disappointed in the first place. So this was all for the benefit of the cameras, then?

Don't be a fool. Why do you think you're here in the first place? She cleared her throat.

"What do you think of our little country?" he murmured, somewhere in her hair. She licked her lips.

"For a place that stresses modesty and taste, there are an awful lot of casinos."

He half snorted, half laughed, then walked through a massive carved door into a foyer. A line of staff dressed in black and white stood, but Akil shook his head.

"Hello, everyone. She's exhausted. Introductions tomorrow," was all he said, and the staff scattered. Tobi took the opportunity to half hide her face in his neck, closed her eyes. Her senses were overwhelmed by that now-familiar sweet spiciness of his skin, completely unaffected by the twelve-hour day. If anything, it had only become headier, more complex.

"You smell good," she whispered, and she felt rather than saw him smile. Fake or not, this was awfully nice and there weren't any cameras here, were there? "Thank you for sending them away."

"You wouldn't have remembered a single one, the way you are now." His voice was rumbling low in her ear. She sensed them crossing a large space, then walking into a lift; he was still carrying her as if she weighed little.

"I think I did all right," she said sleepily.

"Your accent is abysmal, and you kept galloping ahead of me. But, yes," he admitted, the mocking leaving his voice. "You did *splendidly,* not just 'all right.' I was very impressed."

Warmth sparked deep in her chest at his praise; she'd never had any from her father, regardless of how well or how badly she'd behaved. "Thank you."

He grunted in response. They were now moving rapidly down a long hallway; he paused and made a turn, said a command in Djoboran. Tobi, sensing the light changing behind her lids, opened her eyes and peered out.

They were in a large, quiet bedchamber. Enormous windows stretched from ceiling to floor, heavily curtained. The room was dec-

orated in the same opulent style as most of
the buildings she'd seen since her arrival, but
avoided most of the rusts and reds that were
popular. This room's tiling and arched door-
ways were rendered in cool shades of blue and
green, shades that reminded her of the landscape she'd seen when she arrived, the way the
mountains touched the sky, and the lush green
of the land that brushed the sea. Djoboro, she
thought, was as complex as the man who held
her now—in equal parts barren and rich, and
all unsettlingly beautiful.

Akil eased her from his arms atop the coverlet of the massive bed; she actually whimpered as she sank in. The mattress was made
of some material that immediately yielded to
her frame, hugging her body, yet supporting it.
Akil's hands were gentle at her feet, tugging off
her shoes, dropping them to the floor.

"I'm going to get makeup all over the coverlet," she protested drowsily.

"No matter. They'll change it." He looked
tired for the first time since they'd arrived, new
lines about his mouth. He shucked off his jacket,
muscles straining against the snow-white shirt
underneath, and then he was unbuttoning his
shirt, and Tobi was suddenly wide awake.

"What are you doing?" she whispered.

"I'm getting this damned uniform off so I can

sleep." His voice was calm. "And yes, I'll be sleeping with you. Staff gossip like old market women, and it won't kill either of us to cohabit for the time being, regardless of…"

Regardless of if we're sleeping together or not. All thoughts of slumber fled as Tobi half sat up in bed. Her mouth went dry as he pulled his shirt off his shoulders.

In the hazy confusion that came from exhaustion, she registered bronzed dark skin that stretched tight over those heavy muscles; he was leaner without clothes, less stocky, but even more powerful-looking. The little light in the room played over his chest, down his stomach, disappeared into the waist of his trousers; he shucked them next, revealing tight black shorts, legs that were as lean with muscle as the rest of him. Tiredness could not explain why her mouth was dry and why her body was suddenly so tense it hurt.

"Akil…"

He wasn't looking at her; instead he was sighing through his nose, drawing back the coverlet. Tobi's stomach tightened at the prospect of being so close to him. Suddenly, this was too intimate, too much and yet…

"Sleep well, Tobilola," he said, and rolled onto his side, his back to her. It was a wide and formidable back, corded, full of knots under that flawless skin. She wanted desperately to touch it, to press against him, to indulge in his warmth as if she were a cat. She waited ten minutes, watching the breaths lift and lower his back. When they grew slow and regular, when he'd relaxed, she reached out tentatively, touched his shoulder. "Akil."

"Eh?"

"Are you sleeping?"

"I *was.*" The lilt in his voice indicated that he'd been very happily occupied doing so.

"Thank you," she said. That tension had filled her chest, threatened to break out in something as undignified as tears, or something ridiculously sentimental. If he rejected her now she might actually die, she thought, feeling close to hysteria.

She was shocked when he rolled full over, pulling her against him.

"Sleep," he commanded.

"Akil—"

"I remember what happened on the train," he said roughly. It was his first allusion to their kisses that night, and Tobi felt oddly relieved that he said it—so he'd been thinking of it, too! "I won't pretend I don't. I don't want to be alone, all right? But we are *not* dealing with that tonight."

She nodded, and the flash of warmth through her extended from her head down to her toes.

I don't want to be alone.

So this was more than just about those cameras, after all.

The feel of him should have been overwhelming, but instead it was reassuring. Warm. Safe. Despite his arrogance and their squabbling, she'd never felt safer in her life. It was strange; Akil was the first person she'd shared any intimacy with that she didn't feel the need to run from.

Tobi swallowed, then adjusted so that she better fit the cradle of his arms. Her bottom pressed between the apex of his thighs, and she was startled to feel—

"Oh," she breathed, and Akil growled.

"Yes, it's you. I'm only human, after all."

She laughed, and the sound was breathy and unnatural, even to her. "Is it uncomfortable?"

"Quite pleasantly so. Stop moving."

"Why?" She shifted again, and Akil's fingers snaked down lightning-fast to capture her wrists. She made a sound deep in her throat. It was as if someone else had taken over her body. It was part lust, and part fascination at the fact that, well, in *this,* at least, she could make him react.

"Akil…" She lowered her voice, turned her

head. She could not see his face, of course, from this angle, and there was something very sexy about being trapped here, against his smooth, hot skin. He muttered something that could have been a curse and she laughed. It felt so odd to be in such a clear position of power over Akil, but curiously heady as well.

"You're a lot more naked than I am," she whispered.

Everything stilled, reduced to them, close together on that bed; then, he sighed as if defeated and released her wrists. "I should have known this was a terrible idea."

"And yet you brought me here," she pointed out.

"Yes." His mouth tipped up a little. It made this all a little easier, this tacit acknowledgment of what had been burning between them since the very beginning. "You want to be naked, you do it."

Tobi half sat up on the bed; her stomach was churning, and sleepiness was completely gone. She forced herself to meet his eyes, then, before she lost the courage, she pulled her top over her head, her skirt down her hips. The bra came next, and— God, the clasp *stuck*. She fumbled with it like a teenager before finally, impatiently, yanking it over her head. She felt horribly awkward. This had to be the most unsexy striptease ever. Her fingers skimmed the waistband of the thong she was wearing with the first bit of hesitation.

"Stop," he said. "And open your eyes, Tobi."

"I don't want to," she mumbled.

"Ojo," he mocked.

Her eyes flew open indignantly. "You finally learn some Yoruba only to call me a scaredy-cat?"

"It also means 'reign.' I could be calling you a queen."

"Not the way you pronounced it!" She sat up all the way and looked at him, and then she couldn't breathe for a moment because he was looking at her, directly into her eyes, and the look on his *face—*

She scuttled backward, and he laughed. *Laughed.*

"Don't back out now. You started this."

She was hyperconscious of her breasts bouncing on her chest as she scooted back, on the way his eyes rested on them and then on her face, and finally—of the way he was now straining against those black boxers. If he were as large as the shape of him there suggested—

She moved backward again and then there was nowhere to go; she was pressed against the plushness of the velvet headboard and he was kissing her. Hard. It was not an initial kiss; it was a continuation of what they'd started on the train. It was a bruising kiss that told her he was in deadly earnest, and she, Tobi Obatola, was definitely in over her head.

Then his hand curved possessively round one of her breasts, and she lost all coherent thought. It was startling, the way her body surged up to meet his, as if they'd both ceased to be themselves, as if they'd been taken over by some passion both were loath to admit. He made her look at him as his thumbs skimmed her nipples; he spoke low and husky in her ear, and she could not stop the shuddering that went through her body. Unexpectedly, as good as it felt, she felt overwhelmed by emotion. Akil wanted her, yes, and he hadn't wanted to be alone, but there was no tenderness here; she could be any woman with a lush body and warm scented skin. He was enjoying—*this*. He wasn't enjoying *her*.

Unbidden, tears sprang to her eyes; she shut them tightly.

Akil's mouth was making a slow, careful descent down her body, leaving a heated trail where his lips touched. He made a rough sound of appreciation when they grazed her thighs, when he found her warm and sweet and—

"So ready," he breathed out soft against her skin, and he was kissing her there, drawing back when she cried out. "Watch me," he instructed.

No. She'd see nothing but this in her dreams and waking hours and she supposed he knew it. But she bit her lip till it bruised, looked down at the curly dark head hovering between her thighs and let out a shaky breath. Her body was buzzing with want; her nipples were swollen and so tight it was painful at this point. Slowly she lifted her hands to cover the stiff points. It felt good, and would keep her from touching Akil's head, his gleaming bronzed back, tense with muscle.

When his mouth lowered to her again, she vented the breath she was holding on a moan. Minutes faded to nothingness; she concentrated on the ripples of pleasure beginning low at her spine, spreading upward to where her fingers teased her swelling breasts. Akil's full mouth was gentle, languid; his tongue skimmed where she was swollen and wet so precisely that breath cramped in her lungs. Just as the ripples were cresting over into something both new and intensely familiar, Akil lifted his head, pressed his forehead to hers, replaced his mouth with a featherlight pass of his fingers.

"So sweet," he said, and there was a new huskiness in his voice. Tobi tipped her mouth against his hesitantly, tasting the odd sensation of herself on his tongue, and she sighed, then gasped as he slid a finger inside her.

"I want you to tell me what you want," he commanded.

"I—" Tobi's body felt as if it were on fire. *Impossible.* Besides what she wanted, what her heart was beginning to whisper to her in quiet moments since they'd arrived was something she could never say aloud. Not to him. Not after such a short acquaintance, and not after the terms of their deal. She hadn't even dared to say it to herself. But the truth was—even in their tensest moments, she thought of him. And he'd said—he'd said—

She terminated the thought swiftly. That was too dangerous to pursue. What her body cried out for now was much, much safer.

Or was it?

"Akil…"

"Tell me." There were two fingers now, stretching her, applying soft pressure to where she pulsed inside, and Tobi could not talk at all. Instead she bit her lip against the moan that wanted to escape, began to roll her hips against his fingers. Hesitantly at first, but then harder—

He swallowed the broken cry of her pleasure with his mouth, withdrew his fingers slowly as she shook, trying to regain her composure. In the haze she could feel his hands drift slowly up to her breasts, thumbing her still-swollen nipples almost absently. She forced her eyes open.

He was looking directly at her, and she swallowed. Then she reached out herself, placed her hands on his chest.

"I want to touch you," she said quietly, and a muscle jumped in his cheek. The next few moments were an exploration of taut skin, hard muscles, long limbs—all so different from the rounded softness of her own curves. Tobi explored with fingers and lips, noting where his breath caught in his chest, where he held back a sound behind gritted teeth.

"I know I'm not hurting you," she said with a fraction of her old spirit.

He forced out a short laugh. "No, you're not. But I have not done this in some time, Tobilola, and—"

His words trailed to nothing then, for she dipped her hand in the waistband of his shorts, finding him straining, hot, hard, heavy in her hand. He cursed low under his breath, and Tobi arched against him as much as she could, laughing softly against his mouth. Instinct dictated her slow caresses, the pass of her thumb over the tip of him, and when he groaned—

"Not done this in some time?" she said innocently.

That brightness was back in his eyes, eclipsing them, making them as dark as coal. "No. I'm married," he said shortly. Tobi had little time to register this, for in an instant he'd flipped her to her knees and applied a gentle slap to her rear end that made her squeal with shock and excitement.

"Minx," he said, low and hot into her ear, and she could feel him, bare now, nudging against her entrance, which was hot and aching again. "This is entirely your fault."

Tobi responded with a husky sound of her own; she'd never made such a noise in her life, but embarrassment was dissolved by want. His fingers went to the tiny bundle of nerves he'd teased so expertly before and Tobi found herself pushing back against him. Hard.

"Please," she whispered. "Now, Akil." She couldn't think. She couldn't remember that it was her first time with any man, she couldn't remember protection, she couldn't process anything except the fact that she wanted him to fill her. Desperately.

He said something quiet and low as he adjusted himself behind her; then he entered her with one quick thrust.

She gasped as the sting came first, and it was enough to buckle her knees with shock. He hadn't been rough; on the contrary, but it was startling, that sudden feeling of fullness, the swift discarding of the barrier there. She could not help but cry out, a much different cry

from the ones she'd uttered before—and Akil
froze completely. She whimpered a little as she
felt her walls contract, lock him in. Her body
definitely wanted this, no matter how shocked
it was by the abruptness.

"Are you all right?"

She was all right—she'd never been so well in
her life. But she was also very aware of the pain
from that initial thrust, and if it continued—

"I'm—I'm so sorry, Akil, it hurts."

His hands loosened at her hips, and the oath
he uttered reverberated through the bedchamber. Her body, so shockingly, deliciously full a
moment ago, now empty.

CHAPTER NINE

THE DAWN FOUND Akil wide awake, troubled and looking at his young wife. Despite the fact that he felt completely drained, he couldn't have slept even if he wanted to. The pure terror that coursed through his veins every time he gazed at Tobi's face, gentle and sweet in slumber, would not allow him to. Neither did the memory of the night they'd shared.

She'd been a virgin. A *virgin.* And he'd thrust into her that first time like an absolute brute. She'd been so wet, and swollen, and ready, whimpering his name and begging him, in the most becoming matter, after he'd teased her to near madness. He'd positioned her gently on her hands and knees, lightly skimming skillful fingers between her thighs, increasing gentle pressure and parting her downy softness till she arched in a gloriously wanton way, pushed back against him, cried out his name in a soft, broken voice—

He'd done it that way because he didn't want to look at her. He didn't want her to see him, and could not risk the tenderness that made his whole body ache showing in his eyes. And then he'd *hurt* her, thrusting into her like some kind of—

He swallowed. There had been *some* resistance, but he'd been so swift—and she'd barely made a sound, not until she couldn't take it anymore. And then the sound she had made—

"I'm—I'm so sorry, Akil, it hurts."

He'd turned her over rapidly then, seen the tears on her lovely face, the bright red indent where she'd bitten her lip raw. And the arousal had drained from him like water from a sieve.

"Why the hell didn't you tell me!" he'd yelled before realizing that reaction was equally bad; she'd curled up on the bed, absolutely humiliated. And he'd *still* berated her.

"A virgin? That is not information you withhold!"

"I'm sorry—I didn't want you to think that I was—"

"That you were what? That you needed to be treated gently? Tobi, what the hell?"

Panic had seized him, made his words harsh, his voice hard. Tobi had tried to escape, but he wouldn't let her, and after a struggle that involved a hot bath he'd forced her into, she'd cried on his chest before falling asleep in his arms.

A disaster. That's what this had been. And morning was here, soft dancing light on her beautiful face, and he had no idea what the hell he would tell her. He closed his eyes, stomach roiling, and wondered for a moment if he'd be sick. He had spent years cultivating and maintaining hard-edged control. To what end? Manhandling his wife and taking her with all the finesse of a bull in heat?

The self-loathing made his mouth feel bitter. He began easing himself off the bed—and then he froze, because Tobi's eyes were open, and fixed on him. Her lips trembled, a little; she pulled the thin sheet that covered her still-naked body a little tighter to her, and something coiled tight in his stomach.

He didn't look her in the eye. He *couldn't.*

"Good morning," he said, and the timbre of his voice was odd, even to him.

"Akil—"

He shook his head. He didn't want to hear her say anything, not because she didn't deserve to speak, but because he actually felt sick on the inside—and everything depended on his holding himself together. "I owe you an apology. The fact that I had no idea that you were—that you'd never—"

"How could you possibly know that?" Her voice was quiet. "You don't know me."

"No." She was right. He didn't. He'd married a stranger, he'd dared to indulge in sex as—what? Stress relief?—and now he was paying for it.

"I was completely out of bounds."

Tobi laughed incredulously. "If I remember correctly, I begged you to…well, you did exactly what I asked you to! If I couldn't handle it—"

"That isn't the point!" Akil realized just a bit too late exactly how loud he was; the sound of his anguish reverberated in the massive bedchamber. "I lost control," he said after a pause. And by his ancestors, he still hadn't regained it in the presence of this maddening woman.

"Akil. It was the heat of the moment."

"I do not have heated moments." His voice was clipped, brusque.

"I don't understand," she said softly, and sat up in bed.

He closed his eyes against the headache that was forming, and partly against the sight of that damned sheet sliding down again, the firm heaviness of her breasts.

"Do you know why we're here, Tobi?" he said.

"Because you are king." Her voice was soft. "And you're doing an amazing job so far."

Akil squeezed his eyes shut; this could not possibly get any worse. It seemed that every encounter he had with Tobi uncovered another layer of intimacy that he could not afford to have. Not with her. Were it someone he cared for less...

He pushed away the thought with all his strength. "Listen. I've never done this."

"Never had sex, you mean?"

He glared at her.

"Well, what else was I supposed to infer?"

"This is not the time to get *cute*, Tobilola." Akil closed his eyes again. He was no longer warding off a headache; he couldn't ward off something that had arrived and apparently, intended to stay. How could he make her understand? "I have had a few discreet relationships, mostly abroad. But I always knew I would marry. Preferably someone with experience—"

"But you got me, didn't you?"

"Yes," he agreed before he considered how it sounded, then cursed inwardly and opened his eyes. A hurt look had crossed her face.

"I'm sorry about your tragic backstory, but I'm not a child, Akil. If I neglected to tell you about this it was because..." Her voice trailed off.

"Because what?"

"I didn't want you to stop," she said, and her voice was a near whisper.

The two sat together on their large marriage

bed, in a silence that was only broken by faint outdoor noises: birds, the wind rustling the leaves.

"You *cried*," he said roughly.

"Because you were angry. And I was embarrassed." Her face was tight with it now, and unbidden, an image of her came back to him, in vivid, living color. She'd been in that incredibly provocative position, bottom high, thighs apart, and she'd looked back at him, and the hunger on her *face*—

He forced his thoughts to halt because if he could keep his mind from wandering, his body was a little easier to get into line. And he was feeling it stir at the memory, even after all this—

Wordlessly, he slid from the bed. He should be able to avoid this vivid, alluring woman, find plenty to keep her busy.

And at night, when the danger was in them being alone, here in this massive bedchamber, he'd find plenty to keep him busy.

Tobi's mouth tightened, and he realized too late that she'd probably read his mind. This was too much; he was too vulnerable now, too emotional.

"I am your wife," she repeated.

"Yes." He didn't argue with her. It was true, after all—and the more he argued, the more he ran a risk of saying what he'd kept hidden all these years. He needed her to help him become a respected king, and then he needed her to go. Then, and only then, he'd resume control. He stretched, winced when he heard something pop. "My back is a mess of knots."

"That's because you're tense," Tobi snapped. The emotion on her face, thank goodness, was hidden now; this would make it easier.

"I'm going to call for a masseuse. For you. Then we'll have breakfast and I'll show you round the house."

"Fine." If she sounded sulky, she managed to hide enough of it to make him hopeful.

Perhaps he could pull this off after all.

Akil was as good as his word, and ten minutes after he exited, an iron-faced woman with a portable table walked briskly into the bedchamber, hustled a still-naked Tobi off the bed, prodded and kneaded at her muscles until Tobi felt like a pile of goo. The bedchamber had two massive bathrooms on either side; Akil was presumably shut into one. Hers was decorated in soft shades of lilac and blue, and was already stocked with her favorite Jo Malone products. How Akil's staff had discovered these details, she had no idea.

When she emerged from her ministrations, fragrant and calm, Akil stood impatiently in front of a rack of clothing, fully dressed in a simpler version of the linen tunic and trousers that were staples here. "Did you fall in the drain? We're behind schedule."

"I'm not going to let you spoil my mood," she countered. "I've just enjoyed a massage, and I'm so relaxed right now I think I could do a split."

He fought back a smile.

"Day two. Everything has to be perfect." He looked at her, and Tobi's heart sank, despite herself. The man she'd shared a bed with the night before, the man who'd been so absolutely desolate this morning, was completely gone. In his place was the insufferable Akil from the Dubai International Airport, his eyes carefully shuttered of all emotion. "Jamila will be here shortly to dine with us."

"Oh, Jamila," she sighed without thinking, and Akil's mouth twitched.

"Is she giving you a hard time?"

"No, the contrary, actually." Tobi paused. "She's incredibly kind and very helpful. But I simply don't understand how…she just lost her husband. I think I'd be completely nonfunctional if anything happened to you—"

She realized what she was saying much too late, and aborted her sentence, feeling her skin burn in a way that had nothing to do with hot water or exfoliation. Akil was looking at her, a curious softness in his eyes.

"You're a very good person," he said after a long moment. "And so is Jamila. But it hasn't been easy for her. I'm glad you like her."

"I really do."

"Good. Now get dressed," he ordered, a hint of bossiness coming back. "I can't tell you how tired I am already, and the day hasn't even started," he added as if to himself.

Something about his drawn face gave Tobi courage, and she chewed the inside of her lip before stepping up to him, wrapping her arms round him without a word. She did it quickly, with no thought of consequence; he stiffened in surprise, but he *let* her.

"Never mind your hugging nonsense," he said gruffly, but his voice sounded just constricted enough to make her own throat tighten.

"I think you're doing a splendid job," she whispered into his skin. It was easier when she wasn't looking at his face.

"I have no choice." He was pulling away from her now, but his hand lingered at the small of her back. "Thank you," he added, after a moment. "And please, go get *dressed.*"

Tobi appeared ten minutes later, dressed in a soft day dress of brightly patterned *Ankara* that belted at the waist, left her arms bare. He looked at her, nodded approvingly, and headed off without a word.

She said nothing as she walked alongside her husband, nodding politely at the lines of staff awaiting her in the foyer, handed the head housekeeper and butler the gifts she'd brought them—fine chocolate, nuts.

A tour of the house and grounds was next, and Tobi found it impossible not to let her eyes widen with delight, much as she wanted to remain cold, distant. Her new home sat just outside the city, on one of its highest hills, and its construction was like nothing she'd ever seen before. Everything about it seemed to want to embrace the sun: massive windows that let in light from floor to ceiling, skylights, verandas and porches. A balcony the size of a small bedroom with a glass floor was at the highest point of the house, and the view was astounding: the city spread out below them.

There was pride in Akil's handsome face that completely overtook the tension of that morning; he placed a hand on Tobi's back in a gesture that was quickly becoming familiar, pointed to four hills that flanked the city. "Those are the other royal houses." He hesitated for a moment. "Technically, we should be staying at the palace. But I don't—like it. It feels as if I can never have a rest."

"That I definitely understand. But it's beautiful, all of it," Tobi said, a lump coming to her throat. She was queen of all of this? *Temporary queen.* She had to remind herself that this wasn't permanent.

"It is," Akil said matter-of-factly. "It's not a giant like Nigeria, of course. But there are certain problems we've avoided by staying so isolated. And the country's reputation as a tourist paradise is enough incentive to keep it in good shape." He tilted his head. "Of course, you know what our main export is."

"Rubies," Tobi said promptly, and she actually laughed at his expression, despite herself. "And don't praise me for knowing. My sister is a jewelry collector, and she's thrown quite a bit of money your way."

"I'll have her sent some of our finest." He looked at her for a long moment, considering, it seemed; then he reached out and grabbed her hand.

"Come."

Tobi was so startled that she allowed him to tow her down the hall, into the lifts, and back to the main foyer. He led her outside the main entrance, then gestured to one of the two massive pillars in the front of the house. "See that brick?"

She peered at it. Unlike the concrete villas that were more commonplace, the stones of Akil's house were gray and white swirls, almost like marble, with pinkish-red stones of varying size.

She gasped and pressed her hand to her mouth. "Those aren't—"

"Uncut rubies. Yes." A smile played round the corners of his mouth. "The king's house has them in every single stone. That's how plentiful rubies are in our little mines. However..."

His voice trailed off, and he looked at the horizon, his dark eyes hazing over.

"What is it?"

"There's quite a bit of illegal mining. We try to regulate it, but..." He lifted his shoulders. "I don't want this to be a country that exports riches at the expense of its citizens. There's so much of that on the continent already."

The passion in his voice made it deeper, richer. "You intend to reform, then."

"I do."

They were quiet then, but the silence wasn't uncomfortable; it was reflective, heavy with thoughts shared and unshared.

Tobi rested a hand on the pillar. The heavy stone was warm with the heat of a thousand blazing mornings like this one, and seemed to have possessed the spirit of the house's resident:

proud. Upstanding. Immovable. She stepped forward and pressed her cheek to the pillar, closing her eyes. Akil would not let her do this, would not let her lean on him.

She didn't want to lean on him, she reminded herself. This was about getting resources and finding what she was supposed to do. She could not afford to fall in love with this beautiful piece of the world and definitely could not afford to develop feelings for its king, no matter how hard her stomach turned over whenever he fixed those eyes on her face.

"Tobi." Akil's voice held its usual sharpness, but she knew instinctively that it was from concern this time, not irritation. "Are you all right?"

She shook her head, then nodded, knowing full well she must look confused, at best. "I— no. Yes. I mean—" She stared out over the landscape till the blue of the sky and vivid green of the hills began to blur into one. She was inspired by his words; she was touched by the beauty of the landscape, and in some ways, she was envious. Akil so clearly belonged here, whatever the challenges of his position. And she—

"Tobi?"

She looked up.

"I want you to know how essential you are

to this process," he said firmly. "You are going to do well."

Oh. How was it that Akil always managed to steer to the heart of the matter, whatever it was? She swallowed, and was grateful when he seemed not to expect a reply.

"I've also made a decision," he said after a moment. "I'd like you to handle my PR with the team from London."

She stared for a moment, uncomprehending. "What?"

"I have very little patience, which I'm sure you've noticed. You'll deal with them better than I. The briefs, the recommendations—all of it. I'll hear about it once things are finalized, of course, and have the final say, but you did really well in Dubai—"

"I hated what I was doing in Dubai," she countered softly. "It was for the money."

"Nevertheless, you did it well." Akil hesitated, then peered down into her face. "You are my wife, and my partner in this. I believe that you can do it the best. I don't have many people here in my corner yet, Tobi. That will change, of course, but it will take time. This is something I know you'll do well. I believe this sincerely."

There was silence for a moment, then Tobi nodded. "All right."

"Would you like to see the grounds?" he asked, as if nothing had happened.

Tobi took a breath. She wanted a lot of things, but this wasn't the place or the time to mention them. "Very much."

CHAPTER TEN

AKIL DISAPPEARED SOON after the tour, bidding his wife farewell with a kiss—for the benefit of the staff, Tobi told herself sternly. The thought did not stop her from nestling into the crook of his neck for one self-indulgent minute.

This is the last time, she told herself. She needed to concentrate less on him and more on the fact that she was queen and had a memorial service to plan, not to mention her new responsibility to brief the PR team, and the official coronation ceremony, the public-facing one that would celebrate the new administration, set to happen in a month.

She broke out in veritable chills when it came to that. And what sort of a life was she locking herself into by agreeing to do this? She'd married Akil to run from a life devoid of freedom; now she was picturing a future with him because it was impossible not to. He was fast growing tied to the woman she was becoming.

Oh, she wasn't stupid. With every encounter, every kiss, every touch, every conversation, she felt herself wanting him more. But if there was nothing permanent for her here...

Her thoughts were interrupted by David Ashton, the tall whey-faced man who served as head of Akil's PR team. Their briefing that morning was a breakfast meeting, and they sat at the conference table with coffee, fresh fruit and a bewildering assortment of pastries that nobody touched. David smiled at her, a little sardonically, she thought.

"We appreciate your time, Your Majesty."

"It's fine. What is this about?"

It was just as well Akil wasn't there, Tobi thought when the man opened his manila envelope. They were very concerned, David said, about public perception over Akil's estrangement with his father. The former king had been extremely popular, and Akil was being accused in the press of everything from simple callousness to elder abuse.

"Is the public really so blindly devoted to the former king?" Tobi wondered.

"They're more concerned with the fact that Akil doesn't deserve the throne, and he has no regard for tradition or for family," David said blandly. "There have been worse rows behind the scenes, and all have been neatly covered up in the past. It would do the king well to at least attempt the appearance of a reconciliation."

"He's too honest for that."

"Yes. Or too stubborn, it might be interpreted."

Tobi ignored that, even though a part of her secretly agreed. "What do you want him to do?" she asked simply.

"Be seen visiting the old king, perhaps, and making sure he's a part of the coronation celebration. King Al-Hamri knows these things, but is refusing to take the necessary steps. Perhaps you can be of help in persuading him?"

Perhaps I could lose my head, Tobi thought sarcastically. But perhaps she was here for the direct purpose of doing what Akil wouldn't or couldn't do? She chewed her lip for a moment before speaking.

"What if I were to see the old king myself? Spin it that it was arranged at the behest of the king. You could even imply he was there himself, if you wanted." She certainly had done that herself, more than once in Dubai. She particularly remembered a blog that had been written as a result of seeing her in a rooftop garden with one of the ruling sheikh's sons—although the truth was, he'd been leaving as she was arriving. If her socialite life had taught her anything, any story could be created from hearsay and a blurry photo. Akil wouldn't like this, but she'd explain. And it would buy them all some time.

He'd put his trust in her. She had to do this well. And if she could use the skills she'd picked up over the past couple of years, silly as they sometimes seemed, to help him...

David was looking at her thoughtfully. "It's a start," he said grudgingly, pushing back his chair. "I can arrange something for this afternoon, Your Majesty."

"Jamila can come as well," she decided.

"Very well, ma'am."

Akil would understand, she told herself as she broke up the meeting and stood, preparing to go find him. He might even be grateful she'd found a way to solve his problem without involving him at all. And the former king, could he really be that terrible? The old man had been an uncle to her of sorts in the days when her father used to visit, and this was the least she could do to honor the man he'd been, even though his vengeful son seemed determined to wipe every trace of his legacy.

Perhaps fate had brought her here for this reason, to do what Akil could not?

PR has decided it might be a good idea for me to be seen visiting your father. All right? We're setting up something for this afternoon, just a

brief lunch. Jamila's coming, and we'll be pho-
tographed going in and out. Good press.

Akil wouldn't have even seen Tobi's text message were it not for a covert bathroom break.
Standing in the sitting area of the gentleman's
lounge, he felt his body break out into a sweat.

She did *what?* What the hell was she doing?

Without hesitation, Akil headed back to the
main room and abruptly suspended all meetings
for three hours, citing pressing business. He ignored the looks on their faces; this was much
more important. Yes, he knew that Tobi wanted
to help, and yes, he knew that they'd developed
an odd closeness in the past few days, and yes,
he had given her the reins on this, but she had
no right, no right at all.

Adrenaline had him breathing shallowly, and
he forced himself to calm down. It'd been different, years ago, when the only role his father
had played was a seat at his wedding. Now, he
ruled, and if he wanted to keep his sanity, his
father must be kept completely separate from
everything. *Especially* his queen.

The former king was kept in a sprawling es-
tate formerly used as a summer home by his
parents, a secluded place by the sea that was
about an hour out of the city. It represented happier times, and that was why, in a way, Akil had

chosen it for his father's convalescence, if that was the word he wanted. They had spent most of their summer vacations there as boys, and his father was much more relaxed when out of the public eye. He'd drunk less. Spoken to his wife with actual kindness. Looked at Akil once or twice as if he weren't a complete disappointment, and his more violent tendencies...

Akil shoved the thoughts from his mind. He couldn't let them affect him, not if he was to face his father today. Part of him hoped he could grab his wife and make a quick exit, but he knew in his heart that wasn't likely to be the case.

The manservant who met him at the door regarded Akil with a flash of astonishment that was quickly buried under a mantle of professionalism. He bowed low.

"Where is my wife?" Akil said impatiently.

"They are in the moon garden, Your Majesty. If I may announce you."

"No need," Akil said crisply, and walked into the house.

From what he could tell, the place was airy, spotlessly clean, well-kept. Built in a traditional Moroccan style, with open corridors and rooms, high arched entryways for air to pass through, decorated in shades of peach and a brilliant blue that reflected every ray of the sun. He remembered his mother's voice, trailing sweet and clear through the halls, her tinkling laugh. He remembered the way he and his brother's feet had sounded, drumming loud on the tiled floor, of the way they chased each other and slid into the walls.

He walked a little faster.

As had been for years, Akil smelled the garden before he saw it. The moon garden was the house's main showpiece, and he found himself pausing a little to take a breath before entering. The cool green oasis was littered with benches and little stone tables; trees heavy with foliage shrouded parts of it in shadow, welcome pools of coolness in the scorching sun. There were flowers everywhere, all of them white, from all over Africa, heavy with sweet tropical scent. It was in front of a cluster of enormous peonies that Akil found his wife, his sister-in-law and his father.

The years had shrunk him. Out of his royal robes and in a simple striped djellaba worn by many men his age, he hardly looked like the king Akil remembered. He was talking animatedly to Tobi, and Jamila, who'd clearly elected to leave off mourning for the visit, was adjusting the sleeve of her pale green dress and nodding as well.

Akil did not blink; he did not swallow, and he

did not allow himself the comfort of wiping his palms on his hands. Instead he lifted his chin and started forward. He didn't know what was louder, the angry throbbing in his head at the thought of Tobi's actions today or the thudding of his own heart.

More than anything, he was discomfited at the idea the man could still affect him so much. His father hadn't touched him for years by hand, and hadn't spoken a word to him in years, either.

The old man no longer had power over him! Akil squared his shoulders and moved forward with all the arrogance he'd learned from the former king.

"—tell your father he must visit me sometime, it's been too long," he heard him say comfortably. "You were a good girl to come and see me, Tobilola. You'll come to Jamila's wedding, I hope?"

On Tobi's left, Jamila's face gave little away. "Of course she'll come," she said smoothly. "I wouldn't have it any other way, *baba.*"

"Excellent, my daughter—excellent. We just need your mother back, and Akil—"

You're going to get Akil back sooner than you thought, Akil thought drily before pushing aside a delicate fern and stepping into full view of the party.

Silence fell. Tobi's face was equal parts

scared and defiant, and Jamila looked resigned to whatever would come from this, but it was his father who spoke.

"Can I help you, young man?"

Shock, almost visible in its intensity, rippled through the group. Tobi opened her mouth, but Jamila shook her head and placed a warm hand on Tobi's arm, warning her to be silent. "Don't you know who this is, *baba?"* she asked cheerfully.

The visit so far had gone very well, although it had been startling to realize that the old king thought her still a teenager, the impulsive daughter of one of his childhood friends. He'd greeted her as such, spoke fondly of Malik, reprimanded Jamila for not bringing him.

"He's been very busy, though, since I took ill," her father-in-law explained. "And with Akil away…" He would not expand on where Akil supposedly was, regardless the amount of gentle prodding she attempted. Jamila shot her an "I'll explain later" look that Tobi found maddening at best.

Akil away *where?*

"I wouldn't have asked if I knew who he was, would I?" The slightest bit of impatience had entered the old king's voice. "And its's a bit irregular, I think, to show up unannounced."

"Oh, I invited him, *baba*. He's a—friend." Tobi choked a little on the words, and for one wild moment it felt as if Akil would choke right along with her. Jamila looked as if she were holding her breath, and the old king peered into his son's face.

"Ah. I know what that's code for. Welcome, son." And he reached out, took Akil's hand. His face was frozen in disbelief, and partly fury.

"It's an honor to meet you, Your Majesty," he said, more than a little stiffly, and gave one jerk of his head. "I've come to collect Tobi and Jamila."

"Oh, so playing chauffeur, then?" his father chuckled. "If you'd like to—"

Akil did not wait to see what his father would offer; he spun on his heel and left the garden abruptly. Tobi felt the chill down to her toes; Akil was *furious*.

"I'll come another day, sir," she said to the former king, and stood, feeling a fresh wave of pity wash over her. She wasn't even sure he knew how sick he was, but she did know one thing—the man was incredibly lonely. She'd been lonely so much herself she recognized the signs. Sequestered here, with no one but his staff to keep him company, and no visits at all from his only remaining child…

In one last bit of defiance, she bent and kissed

the warm wrinkled cheek quickly, then turned. Akil was already gone, presumably heading for the front door with all speed.

"I'll stay to give him lunch and take the next train," Jamila said quickly, and Tobi suspected the older woman wanted no part of whatever it was Akil would lay on her. She couldn't blame her, either. She reached her husband and waited breathlessly for the explosion, but he didn't say a word. Not when they were in a car on the way to the station, not when they had boarded the royal coach, not when they were served pastries and tea, and not when Tobi brought forth timidly shared nuggets of conversation. It wasn't until they'd left the shore well behind that Akil deigned to lay eyes on her, and when he did his own were as cold and remote as the pebbles on the shore.

"I'm going to assume you were led astray by the PR team and they convinced you to see that man out of goodwill," Akil said, and his voice was as cold as his eyes.

Tobi steeled herself not to flinch. "Actually, Akil, it was my idea. They wanted you involved, and I left you out of it. This would be a great story. He's your *father*."

Akil snorted without changing expression. "Not that it made much difference, he didn't recognize me. He thinks Malik is still alive, and he thinks you're a teenager. He's been told he's recovering from an illness and will return to the capital soon. Which is true enough. He'll eventually go back, in a box."

"But—"

"Don't let sentiment make you a fool, Tobi," Akil said coldly, and that was too much.

"And you shouldn't let your complete and utter lack of it make it hurt you in the long run!" she retorted. "He's an old man, Akil. He's sick. He doesn't have all his facilities, and you've got him shut up in that place, secluded from everyone else—"

"He's in his favorite summer home, where he had happy memories for years, and he's in the care of staff he's known for decades!" Akil's voice rose. "I moved him because us coexisting at the main palace would be completely destabilizing! His mind is gone, Tobi. Do you really think it would be better to break the news of the death of his pride and joy to him? To let him know that he's unfit to rule, and that the son he's despised for years has taken the throne? Do you think it would be good for him to relive that, every day? Your argument is completely refutable and silly."

Silly? Tobi was beginning to see red, and her voice was beginning to shake. "He's a king—"

"A former king," Akil interrupted, his eyes beginning to glitter dangerously.

"—and I stand by the choice I made. It was a small concession that will do you a lot of good, Akil. It will show that, in some way, you do care. That there is some love there, despite your separation."

"Everyone is worthy of care, but love shouldn't be reserved for everyone. He certainly hadn't much for me," Akil added, half under his breath, and more than a little bitterly.

Her throat was thickening with a sudden need to cry. She didn't know why she was so very emotional about this; an impersonal, very rational part of her realized that Akil was right, in some ways. But what bothered her about it, she supposed, was the utter lack of care her husband had for his father. Was he truly so cold, so unforgiving? Could he put those he loved out of sight as well as out of mind so effectively?

After all, he'd cut her off rather effectively before. And though it had no right to, though he'd promised her nothing, the old hurt resurfaced and brimmed.

Akil was peering at her half furiously, half warily, as if he were trying to choose between verbally flogging her or trying to investigate the source of his wife's distress. "I know you did it to help," he said after a long moment.

The anger was still in his voice, but it had dissipated somewhat.

"Right." To Tobi's distress, a tear escaped her left eye, and she wiped at it furtively. Akil silently produced a square of spotless white linen from his pocket and she shook her head. "I don't need it."

"Take it."

She did, dabbed at her eyes.

Akil leaned back in his seat and crossed his arms. His face was formidable. "I don't want you to waste tears on that person."

"I was fond of him as a child, Akil," she whispered, voice muffled by the layer of white fabric. It smelled of him, and she closed her eyes briefly, feeling something in her chest constrict. What was wrong with her? Why was she so emotional lately? "And that memory is all I have to go on. Won't you tell me what happened? I can't make informed decisions unless I know the whole story."

Akil looked trapped and angry and resentful all at the same time for a moment; then he took a breath.

"Maybe. Yes. But not today," he said crisply. "And you will not go back there," Akil said after a moment. His voice was calm; all the concern had gone out of it.

At that Tobi stiffened. "Is that an order?"

"It's a fact." Akil stood to his feet. "We will not discuss this unpalatable subject again as it seems to distress you, but *you will not go back to see him*. Is that understood, Tobilola?"

Tobi gaped. "You are forbidding me to go?"

"You've other things to do, like the pleasant, *simple* task of planning my brother's memorial service, which I'm sure you've neglected in favor of chasing a senile old man. Find a way to solve the problem that doesn't involve him. Or, even better, trust me to turn things around without having to pander to such nonsense!" Akil pivoted and left the car without a further word.

CHAPTER ELEVEN

TWO DAYS. IT took two days before Tobi said a word to him outside of general politeness. Akil told himself he didn't care, stifling the uncomfortable feeling that surfaced whenever he replayed their argument in his head. After all, he had plenty to do.

After the initial ceremonial bits of kingship, there was debriefing. Loads of debriefing. Akil hadn't felt so inadequate at anything since he was in school, the dunce to Malik's genius. He spent nights in his enormous study, where he could be alone, and that was what he wanted the most.

Malik hadn't changed a thing during his brief rule, and just as they'd done upon his arrival, ghosts of who they'd been seemed to hover, mockingly, ready to assess every single thing he did, ready to chant the old man's words directly into his ear.

Who are you trying to deceive?

You can't do this.
You'll fail—as you always did.

He blocked out the voices with every bit of strength, therapy and discipline he'd curated over the past three years. Since leaving, he hadn't failed. Without his family tearing him down, he'd been a success.

He had to be meticulous and thorough in a way he'd never been before he left. As he had in Morocco with his own business, he listened to recordings of that day's sessions, taking his own notes, ensuring he understood every concept before moving on to the next, essentially learning the ins and outs of what his father and brother had had years and special training to master. He ignored the coolness of advisers who probably thought what everyone else did—they'd gotten short shrift from him—and concentrated on the information they provided instead. It took discipline. It took endurance. It took time.

He could make no mistakes whatsoever.

He'd been painted as a selfish idiot by the press already, thanks to this father's years-long PR blitz. He wasn't going to give them any more ammunition. He arrived early, left late and acted like a model monarch.

The entire time, his disagreement with Tobi hovered in the back of his mind, an unresolved thing that made his stomach tighten.

Of course there was no way she'd understand why he'd done what he'd done, why he'd isolated his father from himself. There was no way she'd be able to understand why and how their relationship came to be. Even the thought of explaining made him feel tired. He wasn't exactly eager to expose his past weaknesses. Not to *her*. Were he thinking about it objectively, he'd realize that perhaps he blamed himself, if only a little, for what happened, for not being what his father and brother had insisted on.

Abusers often intimidate their victims into blaming themselves.

The words, spoken by one of the many therapists he'd seen years ago, came to him unbidden now, and he swallowed at the memory. Truth had been hard and long in coming, and he refused to revert. Yes, he'd come back, but to avoid a constitutional crisis, not for either of *them*.

His eye went to a heavy wood-paneled chrome clock as it struck three. The massive thing had been a gift from the queen of England decades ago, and had been here as long as he could remember. Diplomatic trips, that was yet another thing he'd have to navigate. Kingdom issues within the whitewashed walls of the Djoboro palace were one thing; diplomacy was another. And he, as alone as he was now—

Unbidden, an image of Tobi came to his mind during the processional, crouching low to greet the flock of little girls who'd met them there. She'd handled the crowds with such aplomb, and invitations from far and near were pouring in for her. She was pretty, she was photogenic, she said all the right things, even at court.

And he was here, jamming information into the last vestiges of his aching brain, trying his damnedest not to—

There was a soft noise at the door, and Akil looked up sharply. He'd banned everyone from the room hours ago. But the long-legged figure standing in the archway of the royal study was Tobi. She held a tray in her hands.

Akil was more surprised by his bodily reaction than her actual appearance; he started almost violently, and a flush of actual heat captured him from neck to forehead.

"Oh," he said, and got to his feet, feeling remarkably foolish.

Tobi said nothing; instead she walked into the room, placed the tray carefully on the table in front of him, out of reach of the papers he had scattered about. She was dressed more casually than he'd ever seen her, in a pair of cotton sleep shorts that barely reached the tops of her thighs, a blue tank top with a gently scooping neck, and a duster in African style tie-dye that nearly touched the floor round her feet. In the braided rope slippers she wore, her small feet were adorned with small gold rings, and her toenails were polished with a ruby color that matched her fingernails. Her braids were already tucked beneath a turban that matched the duster, and her face was fresh, free of any makeup.

She looked astonishingly beautiful, and he swallowed back a sudden lump in his throat. This was *bad*.

He focused on the tray for a moment; he smelled Djoboran mint tea wafting gently from a glass pot, freshly baked bread, hummus, large dark grapes that looked absolutely bursting with juice, *labneh*, olive oil, creamy garlic sauce sprinkled with chives, and olives.

"I'm not hungry," he said a little gruffly, but Tobi said nothing, only began to decant the tea into the matching glass cups on the tray. "And it's unseemly for you to be trotting about at all hours with trays like a maid."

"Is it simply impossible for you to thank someone decently, without annoyance?" Tobi's voice was sweet and even. "I'm not here to apologize. I've nothing to apologize for. But I have it on good information that you're practically killing yourself these past couple of days."

"And you're here to rescue me from myself then?"

"I do care about you, you know," Tobi said softly. She hunched her shoulders forward as if to protect herself from whatever onslaught was coming, and strangely the sight gave him a pang deep inside. "What you're doing is hard. And I'm your family, whatever our arrangement."

Silence fell while Akil digested that piece of information. Tobi was still focused on the tray, pushing the tea and then a loaded plate of food at him almost shyly. She still wouldn't meet his eyes.

Akil exhaled slowly, then sat.

Tobi nodded, gathered the folds of her duster round her and turned to go, but Akil found himself speaking. The words came out halted and reluctant, but they were sincere.

"Perhaps... I was too harsh. Please—sit. If you want," he amended. He didn't quite know how it'd come about, but Tobi in a single stroke had dissolved the irritation of the past few days. It was disarming. He never seemed to be able to stick to a resolution when it came to his feelings for her.

"I used to do this for my father and his guests when I was a girl," she said, and finally looked at him, offering him a small smile before easing herself into one of the upholstered chairs near the desk. She waved off his offer of anything but tea. "Jamila and I have an engagement at one of her patronages tomorrow morning, and you should see the dress I've got to wedge into." The corners of her mouth lifted. "Jamila seems to be living vicariously through me, since she's got to wear black for the next year."

"You should be sleeping, then."

"It still feels odd, our room. It's so large."

And empty. There was no censure there, at least none that was deliberate, but Akil felt guilty. She was here because of him, and he'd allowed his own anger to get in the way of supporting her. He'd left voluntarily, but Tobi was a true stranger to Djoboro. And impulsively, he'd acted exactly like the people he had issues with. *Not very kingly behavior.*

He looked her full in the face for the first time since she'd come in. It was as drawn and tired as he felt, and there were faint hollows beneath her eyes.

"Eat," he said gently. "If your clothing is too tight tomorrow it'll only spark pregnancy rumors, which, trust me, is a good thing."

"Oh, goodness." She looked rather ill at the thought, pressed a hand to her abdomen.

"Is the thought so repulsive?"

"I'll pass on that one." She shuddered. "And I think I'll take that plate, after all."

Akil filled it silently. It was a companionable silence this time, and one that was oddly comforting. He found himself looking at the young woman in front of him with her head bent over bread and oil, and an image flashed through his mind, unbidden, then another, and then another, like a montage on a movie set.

Tobi, round with his child, soft and warm with love both given and received. A baby, round-cheeked, with her smooth skin and his dark eyes. The three of them in Djoboro, looking out through the enormous palace windows that flanked every corridor, showing their child his country. Their country.

The images faded as quickly as they'd come, and he was back in the dimly lit study, eating quietly with his wife. They would have to remain images, he supposed. There was no bearing on them in real life, and Akil was never one to believe in fairy tales.

Eventually, Tobi's head began to nod. When it nearly hit the table, Akil laughed and suggested they go to bed.

"Come up," he said, and his voice was heavy with compassion. "I promise, no funny stuff tonight. Just sleep." He did not, thank goodness, refer to his father, or to her visit. He kept up a steady stream of one-sided conversation as they walked slowly to the lift, and took her up to their floor.

Sensation was reduced to the feel of his large, warm hands on her body, stripping her gown and jewelry from her, rubbing her feet, tucking her into a bed with fresh sheets that smelled of lavender and lemon. He pulled off his own clothes, slid in bed beside her, pulled her into the warm wall of his chest.

"Tobi, thank you," he said, and his voice was quiet. Humble, almost. "Everything you have done has been in my support. I recognize that."

Tobi shut her eyes tight, fighting against the roil of emotion that came without fail whenever Akil was being close to gentle with her, and forced a smile that she hoped was casual. "It has been fine. It's…interesting, interacting with everyone. Kingmaking is quite different in Nigeria, and yet some things are exactly the same."

"All the diplomatic sycophancy, I suppose."

"It's more than that." She looked down at her hand, where it splayed on the snow-white sheets. "I was seven, perhaps, when the old oba of our town died. I remember my father's ascension clearly."

"Tell me about it." Akil's voice was mellow, but it was alert. He shifted so that his chest made a warm muscled bed for Tobi to lie on; she closed her eyes, speaking round the slow, steady beat of his heart.

"When the old king dies," she said softly, "the first thing they'll do is deny it. There are a lot of rituals involved, mysteries, they aren't public knowledge. No one, aside from those privy to such things, lays their eyes on the king's body, not even his wife or children. The oba is buried in a secret place, and then, well. There's a lot of bidding, behind the scenes, sometimes."

"Kings aren't put there by birth?"

"Sometimes they are, and it's very straightforward. But there are always other royal families, someone else who can make a claim. And the kingmakers, who are appointed by our old deities to name the new king, they hold supreme power. They are the ones who can hear the voice of the oracle, can tell us what the gods want."

"I thought you went to Catholic school," Akil said, but his voice was interested. It was new for Tobi, this sort of quiet conversation. Her father, sister, stepmother and brothers had never been ones to have serious conversations with her; she'd always been Tobi the troublemaker, Tobi the trickster. Since she'd come to Djoboro, it was the first time she'd ever been given any great responsibility. Akil had recognized her ability as well as her longing to be taken seriously.

It felt amazing, to be honest.

Tobi laughed. "This has nothing to do with Catholicism. It's tradition."

"Well, it's put you in good stead." Akil's voice rumbled in the dark. "Were I the jealous type, I'd be very much so. You've charmed the country, Tobi—we make a formidable team. And I haven't forgotten what you said—we're rebuilding what was burned, to make it more beautiful."

We make a formidable team. I haven't forgotten what you said. Had she ever received that sort of praise from anyone in her life, even Kemi? In just a few short days, she'd found a place where she was important, where what she did mattered. She was somewhere where her past had no bearing on what people thought she was capable of. And, despite his ill temper and myriad issues, Akil had given all of this to her. Part of her felt truly pathetic for her thoughts veering toward this direction in the first place, but it was true.

Tobi blinked hard against tears that welled suddenly. It was funny, she'd never cried in all her years of captivity at home, never at all, but she seemed to do little else lately. She stiffened when Akil half turned her and impulsively nosed her face, not wanting him to discover, but he'd already tasted the wet, the salt.

"Oh, Tobi," he said, and the compassion in his voice made her heart hurt. "You must be tired out of your mind. Why are you crying?"

Good question. She was crying because all of this ultimately had an expiry date; she was only useful to Akil in establishing his kingship, and once that was over, once he'd won over his people…

"I'm trying to get used to the idea that you soon won't need me anymore," she whispered. She might as well be honest, as long as she was in this situation.

Akil's arms grew rigid for a fraction of a second, then he sighed. "Tobi—"

"Don't worry, I'm not in love with you." Possibly another lie, if she were honest with herself, but she could not afford that, not now. "I'll take the money and go."

He grunted. "It sounds rather crass to say it like that, Tobi."

"But that's what it is, isn't it?" She swallowed, hard. "I agreed to this bargain, and you're going to get what you want—"

"You will as well," Akil said, a note of warning entering his voice.

"I know. Trust me, I know. But—all this…"

"All what?"

"All this." Tobi pushed back against him, then sat up. She couldn't see him in the darkness of their bedroom, and that made her feel safer somehow. "You acknowledging me, and praising me, and holding me, and kissing me—"

"Tobi."

"We're here in bed, and we're both naked, and we're not having sex," she said, her voice breaking a little. "Don't you see what that means?"

"That's because you're tired. And besides, we've only had sex once—"

She shook her head. "I—no, Akil. What we're doing now—that's what lovers do. But I know this isn't about anything but the kingship, and I know you'd have nothing to do with me if it weren't for it. I keep telling myself this, over and over. And yes, I'm tired, and I never stop hearing Jamila's chattering in my head, but I just don't know—"

It was too overwhelming suddenly, and she wrapped her arms round herself, trying to contain the unexpected wave of pain that rushed in. Days of ignoring her own vulnerabilities, her own desires, had culminated in this: a veritable breakdown in front of the man who was responsible for it all.

No, she corrected herself. *He's not responsible. I am.* She'd come here of her own free will, Akil's demands aside. She'd allowed him to kiss her, to touch her, to take the virginity she'd maintained for—what reason? The passion between them was more than lust, at least on her side.

"You should have left me in Dubai," she mumbled, and lay back down, curling herself up in a ball so tight her limbs ached. She heard Akil sigh and lower himself next to her.

"Perhaps I should have. I don't know what to say," he admitted finally.

Where the hell is this going to end up? She wanted to cry out, but she pressed a fist to her mouth instead. She'd given up enough of her dignity tonight. But she needed to know. So she could protect herself, if nothing else.

"Tobi," he said after a moment. "Please try to understand." He took a breath; she felt it, warm and gentle, caressing her shoulder. "I do care for you on some level—how can I not? You're brilliant, bright, absolutely fearless. In some ways I wish I were more like you. But, Tobi, I know my own shortcomings. I know where I come from and how I was raised. And there's no way I can be anything to you but a disappointment in the long run. This job—it takes people, steals their souls. You weren't born to it. I'm trying to protect you."

Tobi closed her eyes. Yet another man who'd denied her what she needed the most by trying to protect her. Were they all like this? And yet he was still talking. He moved forward, drawing her back into the circle of his arms, his front to her back, speaking in those same oddly dispassionate yet gentle tones.

"If this is too hard, if it helps, we can try and separate sooner—"

"No," Tobi whispered. Separation at this point would only hurt worse. He already knew every inch of her body, and she craved him like a drug.

If she didn't have anything else, she'd still have that.

She turned around, identified the bit of shadow that must be his face, leaned forward. Her kiss landed on his cheekbone; she found her way to his mouth, made a soft sound deep in her throat as she kissed him.

"I'm tired," she said after they drew apart, "and possibly hormonal."

"I understand," he said simply, and that was all he said. He was frowning, as if he were trying to decide something—and then, in a split second, he opened his mouth.

"I'm not trying to provide excuses," he said. "But you're a good person, and I just want to explain."

"Explain?"

"Yes. This is all tied to my past, Tobi—there

is much you don't know. It's complicated, at best. I know you want to make peace. I appreciate it. But what I've done is the extent of what I can do. I'll allow the visits, at any rate. But that is all."

Tobi nodded at the concession, something tightening in her throat. "You can tell me about it, you know."

Akil's grip tightened on her, and his voice came, gentle in the saffron-scented darkness.

"I know. And I will, perhaps. But—not tonight, Tobi."

She didn't answer; there was nothing in the room but her quiet breathing, and Akil spoke after several beats. "So, what was it like for you after?"

"After…?"

"After your father took the throne."

Oh. Tobi was so surprised by the question she turned her head. Akil had never shown a more than rudimentary interest in her past before, and it was startling. "It was odd," she said after a moment, "knowing he was so important. It was fun at first. We lived in the palace, went to the best schools. He married again, and we were fortunate, his second wife was very kind to us."

Akil grunted.

"Then, after my sister Kemi became a teenager, things were a little harder. She was—kid-

napped while out with friends, held for ransom."
Tobi licked her lips. She still remembered that
day, the palpable terror in the air, the way her
stepmother kept running to the bathroom, her
delicate stomach disturbed by fear, the family
clustered round her father's phone, listening
to the demands of the kidnappers over speak-
erphone, to the man's rough voice describing
with glee exactly what he planned to do with
the teenage princess, should his demands not
be met. "It was awful. When they did get her
back, there was an—altercation—and a man
was shot and killed. Kemi was shot, too, and it
crippled her arm."

Akil said nothing, but she could feel the tension in his body; he was listening to every word.

"We were virtually on lockdown after that.
My father took us out of school, kept us in the
house, except for mandated outings where we
had to take a full security escort. My sister actually met her husband on a state trip—I made
her sneak out with me to a nightclub, and there
he was."

Akil chuckled. "You didn't meet anyone that
night?"

"I ditched Kemi to go to a party at the local
university. I don't think she's forgiven me to
this day." She smiled at the memory. Kemi had
gotten pregnant that night as well with her little

nephew, Ayodele, a bit of information she decided to keep to herself for now. "My father was so horrified at that state of affairs, he sought to make me 'another man's problem,' as he put it, as soon as he could—that's where you came in. He thought a great deal of your father."

"And mine of yours," Akil admitted. His lids were lowering; his face was growing slack with impending sleep. Tobi wrapped her arms round him, laid her head on his chest and closed her own eyes, reveling in the tenuous bond that they'd formed, at least for tonight. She could see the dawn pinkening the sky in the large window opposite the bed; they would have to be up in a few hours, anyway.

It was time to rest, for there would be much to do tomorrow, and even more in the days to come.

They had a royal house to rebuild, and she would put her heart into it for as long as he needed her.

Finding herself was a nice bonus.

CHAPTER TWELVE

"You're ready for the memorial service? You're *sure?"* Akil clarified, looking suspiciously at his wife where she sat opposite him at the breakfast table, dressed demurely in a pale green dressing gown, embroidered with white around the hem and sleeves. He hadn't placed any restrictions on her nightwear, but since that first disastrous night in their suite, Tobi had quietly switched to nightwear that was pretty, but the opposite of sexy: long-sleeved pajama tops and loose bottoms, dressing gowns, nightgowns with matching robes. He supposed she was trying to dress for the new role she'd taken upon herself.

Too bad it didn't work. On the worst nights when he closed his eyes he could see her full mouth curved up into a mocking smile, the gleam of her skin against the white of the pillows on his bed, her breasts thrust upward, nipples jutting out, puckered and ready for his mouth. It would have been easier, as well, had he not known exactly how tight and hot she'd been, pulsing hard around the length of him...

"Akil?"

He blinked. There it was again, that soft and dulcet voice she'd been using lately. They hadn't argued once since that night in his study; she'd been acting like the ideal wife. She spent a great deal of time with Jamila, shopping, attending affairs of state in his stead, even going as far as to help his sister-in-law move her extensive holdings to her new royal home at the edge of the city, and unpacking things with her own hands.

"She's a good girl," Jamila said in her weekly reports to Akil, and he knew that was high praise from the former queen. When Akil mentioned it she tucked her braids behind her ear and looked up at him with an expression that was *almost* shy.

"She's important to the royal family, so she is to me as well," she said quietly.

The words hung between them, heavy, loaded with a meaning that he was unwilling to explore. Then Tobi cleared her throat and scuttled from the room, and the moment was lost.

Thank goodness.

At night, he'd find Tobi bent over a language book at the old-fashioned secretary in the sitting area of their bedchamber, head wrapped in enormous headphones, sounding out greetings and pleasantries in Djoboran that were awkward on her tongue. There were flash cards with the members of parliament written in her bold hand that tumbled out of her purse.

In the evenings, he found himself eager to spend time with her, speaking about his work and his hopes and dreams for future projects. Tobi was bright and innovative, he found, and an avid listener. She had a talent for identifying the heart of a matter and pulling out objectives; her mind was like a heat-seeking missile, worming straight to the source and identifying solutions. It was she who mentioned a project that her father had successfully run in Nigeria years ago, providing grants to local drillers who wanted government backing to start their own businesses. It greatly reduced unregulated drilling and black- market sales in that area, because the government had handed the locals the means to success, and created a ready-made workforce at the same time.

"It might work here, too," she'd said simply, toying with the end of her braids in a gesture he'd grown used to as one of her tics. They'd been lunching on the veranda, and Tobi had been staring out at the landscape. "This is a monarchy—it's getting older. It's maturing. Changing."

She had his interest. "Tell me more."

"My father is a king. He gave me everything I wanted, except freedom to be my own person, and I finally started sneaking around to do it. That might be what's happening here. If people get support from you, if you let them know that you *trust* them to be independent—"

"Then we win in the long run," Akil said slowly. "Talent stays in the country. It's a thoroughly modern model, Tobi."

"I wanted to help." She couldn't look at him, and Akil suddenly wanted her to. Desperately.

"Tobi?"

Reluctantly, as if pulled by some unseen force, she turned her face. When her eyes met his they flickered to his mouth, then back up as if she'd caught herself doing something wrong. He took a moment to drink her all in: full lips, long lashes, all the loveliness he tried to forget existed, most of the time.

"It seems odd, not to be arguing with you," he murmured.

She did smile then, a little sarcastic twist of the lips. "I'm trying to be good. I've got a great deal of money riding on it, after all."

Akil had no idea why that statement affected him the way it did, but he found himself drawing back. "Indeed you do."

Tobi's fingers returned to the end of her braids. "I was thinking, I'd like to throw a party.

Not what you're thinking," she said, before he opened his mouth. "It'd be a formal banquet, for the Royal Council. I think it would be a nice gesture before the coronation. I also thought it might be nice—to tie your brother's memorial with it."

She was right. "I'd intended to send them some gifts," he admitted, leaning back. *To celebrate hell freezing over.*

Tobi shook her head. "That's nothing compared to entertaining them in your own home."

"They may not come," he said darkly.

"An invitation from their monarch? All of them? I seriously doubt it. They're snobbish, but they're not crazy."

He grunted. He wasn't so sure, and really hadn't given a toss until then—what were they going to do, take the crown from the only living heir because they resented his exit three years before?

"They know they need to make peace, it's for the good of the Crown, after all. Let them see how you've grown up and how much you're willing to entertain statecraft," Tobi entreated.

She was right. He didn't want to admit it, but she was right.

"I think, perhaps, a week from today." She tilted her head, and his fingers itched to touch the soft arch of her neck. He knew from experience that she'd tense deliciously and begin softening against him. He reached out, brushed the backs of his fingers on that tempting patch of skin, and yes—she tensed with a gentle intake of breath.

"You're just full of good ideas, aren't you?"

"It's hardly a good idea. You know what to do. You're just too stubborn to do it."

"That is true." Akil allowed a rueful smile while still stroking her skin. He could see the rapid rise and fall of her chest. He knew it was a terrible idea, but he couldn't help himself. He could not have stopped himself from drawing his wife to him any more than he could have stopped the earth's rotation. It was want, pure and simple, and the soft curse she uttered before lifting her arms up to his neck was one of response, not denial.

"Akil, *please*," she said, and he cradled her face in his hands, kissing her deeply. All that mattered in that moment was how soft her lips were, the sweet slide of her tongue against his, and pleasing her.

They kissed like lovers, with all the sweet hesitation of something new, heady, real. Any reservations in Tobi seemed to have melted away completely in those first few moments, and she was mewling soft and desperate against his lips, his neck. He hadn't even touched her beyond cupping her face, but the way she was *squirming*—

They'd reached a point, he thought a little hazily, where they could freely admit how much they wanted each other, and the throb beginning in his lower regions was beginning to surpass everything else in importance.

"Do you want this?" he found himself rasping out in a voice that sounded *nothing* like his.

She laughed, and for the first time in weeks she sounded like her old self, arrogance mixed with incredulity. "Of course I do. But—" She squeezed her eyes shut, paused to whimper when his lips connected with a particularly sensitive spot on her neck.

"But what?"

She forced her eyes open, and lust began to erode at the edges of the tenderness; her pupils were blown wide with arousal. "Not here," she said, and pulled away from him, biting her lip so hard he was sure she'd leave a mark. He took a ragged breath of his own.

"Lead the way," he said.

They weren't going to make it, Tobi thought almost wildly.

She and Akil were somewhere in the deserted hallway that led to their bedchamber, and his big, hot hands were everywhere. He'd completely dispensed with control, and that unleashed something in Tobi she'd been suppressing in all these weeks of being his wife, the wife he wanted. He'd stopped her at least three times to kiss her hard, eat up her whimpers and moans with the softness of his mouth, divest her of various articles of clothing; her dress there, buttons scattering across polished tile. Her bra, twisted over her head, left in a stairwell.

The lace underwear she wore took the longest to remove; he pressed her hard against the bedroom door, hooked his fingers in the sides, worked them down inch by inch until she was trembling with need.

"I'm not going to beg," she said through her teeth.

"I think this might happen before we even get inside," he said, his voice raspy and low. Ripples of pleasure went through her even at just the *suggestion*—

"Akil—" she gasped.

"Quiet, for once," he said, laughing low, and before she could protest he was on his knees. He used his fingers, his tongue, nipped and soothed, held her firm, right where he wanted her, until her resolution not to beg was a thing of the past. When their position grew too awkward, when she wanted to arch her back, his strong arms lowered her to the floor. And oh, she begged, threw dignity away with the last of her clothing. She did it in soft little whimpering gasps that ended only when that hot, wicked tongue of his swept *directly* over where she wanted him most—

Explosions. Stars. All the clichés. She was boneless, draped uselessly against the floor, leg dangling over his shoulder. And he was withdrawing from between her legs, looking very pleased with himself.

She was too wrung out to feel irritated; she rolled half over, mostly to shield her face. If he said something sardonic she'd die. But instead he reached out and touched her cheek.

"Are you all right?" he whispered, and then he stretched out beside her, drawing her into his arms. She could feel the length of him on her back, hard and pulsing; in answer to the question she rotated her hips, delighting in the pull, the ache.

"I want you," she whispered.

"Not here," he said with the barest note of laughter in his voice. He was up on his feet in a moment, and when she stood as well he swept her into his arms with as much ease as he'd shown that first night he'd carried her over the threshold. Moments later, when she was sinking into the softness of the mattress and he was slowly, sweetly making love to her with hands and mouth and finally, *finally* filling her aching emptiness with slow, warm thrusts, it was hard to remember how to breathe, or which way was up. And in the midst of it all was something else, something that sparked bright as flame, and yet filled her with complete despair.

She wasn't in love with him yet; she was too pragmatic for that. Or at least she thought she was, and had the self-control to keep her feelings for him from turning into anything else. But this—this wildness, this emotional surge— this was completely out of her hands, something untamed and unexpected. She had no idea how to stop except to stay away from him, and that was impossible.

Air was crushed from her lungs, and she swallowed hard.

She was in trouble.

CHAPTER THIRTEEN

TOBI WORKED HARDER at the party for the Royal Council than anything she'd ever worked at in her life, and felt a heady pleasure at the way it was all coming together. Along with the ever-present Jamila she consulted with party planners, PR people, even her older sister, Kemi, whose parties were written up in Abuja's society pages even more than those of the first lady herself. She reacted with shock at her little sister's first call.

"*Akil* has you doing this? What did he find out about you? Who'd you kill?"

"Whatever." She glanced over her shoulder to where she could hear the sound of the masseuse, pounding her husband's muscles in the privacy of his bathroom after a morning of lovemaking; he was late to parliament, something that was nearly unheard of. She was putting off her own shower and getting dressed. She'd never admit it to Akil, but she loved the pull and burn that came after vigorous sex with him, his salt on her skin, the tang of him on her lips. She cleared her throat and wrapped herself in the coverlet on the bed. "It was my idea."

Kemi's response to that was dumbfounded shock. "You hate those things. You used to sneak out of Daddy's—"

"I've thrown dozens of parties!"

"Not *this* type of party."

"I know. I *know*." Tobi pulled the coverlet completely over her head. "I want to do it. For Akil. I need to know what to do."

Her sister grunted in amazement. "Well— miracles still happen! Simplicity is key. Think about what would be pleasantest for your guests, not yourself. Luxury is felt in the details, pretty surroundings, smiling hosts, excellent food and wine. You've got to make them never want to stop eating."

Tobi obediently took notes on her phone, then made the same call to her stepmother, her father's senior wife. *She* almost fainted at the thought of her stepdaughter willingly hosting a royal event, but by the time she hung up, Tobi felt confident that she'd be able to pull off the event of the season and give her husband a human side that the men and women of the council would appreciate. He was already proving himself to be a faithful leader, serving his country through his economic work.

Now they would see the man, one who despite her fears, she grew closer to every day. She saw him when he was proud, remote and kingly in ceremonial dress, presiding over court; she also saw him when he was sitting huddled over his papers at two in the morning, mouthing the notes for the day, eyes blurry with little sleep. She came to respect both sides and was determined the people would as well.

He would win them over. *They* would win them over.

Akil spent the morning of Tobi's party holed up in his study, doing his best to avoid the virtual army of planners, workers and installers that had swarmed his residence since five that morning. Tobi had crept from the circle of his arms at about three, and presumably was somewhere in the din. Akil plugged in the best noise-canceling headphones he owned, hunched his shoulders down and worked. Since Tobi had mentioned the mining program weeks ago, he hadn't been able to get the idea out of his head. He'd researched similar programs in other countries, and even went as far as to call her father for advice. He'd been surprised and demanded at first to know if his daughter was behaving herself, then reacted with surprise when he'd told him what it was for.

"Tobi told you that?" He laughed. "I had no idea she had anything in her head besides makeup, dresses and raising my blood pressure."

Then you don't know her. Akil had bitten his tongue, taken the information he wanted, and ended the call as quickly as possible. Tobi was an extraordinary young woman, beautiful and intelligent. It nettled him that her upbringing had quite possibly pigeonholed her into thinking she was no better than parties, reality shows. Hell, even being married to a person like *him,* as much as he was enjoying it.

He closed his eyes. He didn't do it often when he thought of Tobi, because the gesture inevitably recalled images of her, taut and damp with perspiration and writhing beneath him. His hunger for her grew every time they had sex, and she shed a little more of her inhibitions with each encounter. Even thinking of it now in this casual way made his body cramp with need.

Akil shifted uncomfortably, then reached for the glass of ice water sitting on his desk. He was unused to this level of want when it came to any woman, and he knew on some level that this was due to intimacy, not lust. He wanted to be close to Tobi, but sex was the only thing he'd allow. Even the thought of letting her in, giving her the type of power he'd never allowed anyone, *ever*—

He couldn't afford it. Especially not if he planned to set her free.

He was drunk off her heady sweetness and his years of self-imposed celibacy, he told himself. Tobi had to go—it was better. He would not have her destroyed by the same system that made him what he was. The deal would be upheld.

He would admit, only here, when he was alone, that perhaps, after all, he'd miss her.

Akil was startled from his musings when his door opened, then irritated when he saw the time. He'd spent a good part of an hour daydreaming about her, for God's sake. His frown intensified when he saw that it was Tobi, but something in his chest leaped up, a little sunburst of warmth. Her braids were gathered into a messy topknot on her head; she was dressed in a T-shirt that showed off a sliver of taut stomach. She was frowning.

"Here you are," she said accusingly. Akil leaned back in his office chair, shooting her his best indolent look.

"Where else would I be?"

"You're supposed to be getting ready!" She glanced down at the small digital tablet she held, expression agitated. "The barber's already here, your masseuse arrives in an hour, and—no. No, don't get up, and do not come over here, unless you're planning to go out the door and meet—"

She was already softening, already sighing, and fell completely quiet when Akil kissed her.

"Calm down," he said simply.

"I can't," she said, and tried to step back, but he held her fast. That delicious floral scent was rising from her skin, and he was already—

"No," she said forcefully, as if she read his mind, and he laughed and released her.

"Sit down and have a drink."

"No." She scowled. "You need to come with me."

"Drink first," he wheedled. "I'll tie up the loose ends on this report, and we can leave together. You need a drink. You look manic."

She faltered, then sighed. "Fine. One drink. Quickly. And you keep your hands to yourself."

He crossed over to the bar, decanted a finger of whiskey into a glass, handed it to her. Tobi made a face and took the tiniest sip, and he laughed. "We've neglected this part of your education."

"I know how to drink it. I just don't like it." Tobi set the offending glass as far from her as she could manage. "Give me rum. Something sweet."

He sighed but filled her request, and the two

sat quietly together, sipping their drinks. Tobi's eyes were bright and not quite focused on the wall art she was staring at. Akil cleared his throat after a moment.

"I don't want you to think that all my grumbling means I'm ungrateful," he said after a moment. "This will do much for my profile."

"And if I know how to do anything, it's how to throw a party," Tobi said drily, crossing her legs. "Not that you'd believe it to listen to my stepmom. She simply can't fathom that my socialite lifestyle might relate in any way to the high-society posturing she enjoys so much."

Akil smiled, and they sat in silence for a moment, cradling their glasses in their palms. "You didn't enjoy it when you were home?"

"I hated it," she said so emphatically that he smiled. "Sneaked out every chance I got from state events. It wasn't the parties themselves, I think—it was the company, and the fact that I was there just to be on display."

"You found your own ways of having fun, though." His mouth tipped upward.

"Oh, yes. I made sneaking out to clubs an art form."

"And you never were caught?"

The smile faltered a bit on Tobi's face. "Oh, I got caught often enough. Usually it was an enterprising housemaid who wanted to get on my father's good side, or the guards I bribed slipped up and forgot to pick me up on time." Her brow grew furrowed as she remembered. "My father had a good firm hand with the *koboko*—"

"*Koboko*?"

"Cane. The type used to drive goats," Tobi said, shaking her head at the memory. "He never hesitated to use it. But I was as stubborn as an old goat—and beatings never stopped me, so he found more creative ways to keep me under his thumb. Punished my maids, punished my older sister." She opened her mouth, then closed it. She didn't really like talking about her father, or those times, but there was something about Akil and his actual interest in her words today that made her want to speak more.

"I'm not defending his…methods," Akil said after a pause, "but I can see why he would want to keep his daughters safe."

"It's a justification for trying to control us," she said briefly. "I'm glad I got out."

Akil grunted, still looking at her with that mixture of curiosity and admiration on his face. "You are an extraordinary young woman," he said briefly.

"I've hardly done anything."

"You've managed to maintain your spirit," Akil said, "which is more than I can say for Malik. His entire personality was built, shaped, curated around the needs of the Crown. I couldn't do that, so I had to leave."

"Do you ever regret the path you've taken?"

He was silent for a long moment before he spoke. "My father abused me for years, Tobi. Mentally, physically, in every way you might imagine. He resented me for my mother's failings, and later, for my own. I'm not sure he ever cared for me. And Malik——" He took a breath. "My break with him will always hurt more than the one with my father. I told him everything on the eve of my seventeenth birthday. I couldn't take it anymore, wanted to kill myself. He laughed, Tobi. Derisively. He didn't believe a word I said, not after how I'd behaved over the years. He accused me of showboating, of seeking attention——"

Tobi covered her mouth with her hand.

"Yes." Akil nodded. "It was then I became determined to leave. My father was a skillful liar, and Malik, unfortunately, was caught in his web fairly early. Neither of them would have been an ideal person to sit on the throne, but I am different." His eyes were suddenly fixed on her, and so fierce that Tobi leaned back. "I am ready to serve my kingdom for as long as it needs me, but it has to be *my* way."

It was such a passionate declaration that Tobi felt a stab of envy—she'd never found anything to care about as fiercely as he cared for his country. Her father had never engaged her with the work that he did, had never thought her thoughts were worth anything.

She glanced at her feet, where the tips of her toes gleamed ruby red. "You shamed me a bit," she said quietly. "I've managed to escape, but I haven't done much for myself—or for anyone else. Until I came here, that is."

"Your tendency toward self-pity is tiresome," Akil said drily. "What do you call the program you were trying to implement? It's going to be successful beyond your wildest dreams— just wait. It's hardly the end of your life," Akil added, and he offered her a smile that was almost kind. "Besides, you're helping me. And as my wife, my queen, you will have access to the world. You will have access to everything you want to learn, and you will be able to take up any cause that you wish. Say the word, Tobi. I will make it happen."

He was offering her the world, and Tobi felt her heartbeat quicken at his words, as well as the intensity that pooled deep in those brandy-dark eyes. He was offering her the world, but he would never offer her himself, and Tobi wasn't sure that it was enough.

Akil's voice broke into her thoughts. "It seems appropriate to tell you now that I'm implementing the program you suggested," Akil said after a moment. "I'd like to give you full credit. And I'd like you to head the committee, if you will?"

Surprise crossed his wife's lovely face. "Me? I'm not an economist."

"Luckily, I am." He allowed the corners of his mouth to tilt up. "And you're something far more important—you know people, and you think about what's good for them from a human standpoint, not just an economical one. You're interested in people, in their needs. And that—well. That will make you a splendid leader, any-where you find yourself."

Tobi was staring at him as if she'd never quite seen him before, and the emotion on her face was something *he'd* never seen before. She set down her glass and crossed her arms over her chest, hunching her shoulders forward, resting her elbows on her thighs. He took a sip, tilted his head, waited. He was a patient man; he could not drag it out of her.

"I don't know what to say." Her voice was quiet.

He lifted his shoulders. "You don't have to say anything. I just wanted you to know that about yourself. You can do something worth more. Don't take that first failure as an indica-tion of inability."

"You're assuming a lot," Tobi said mildly, but

she did not correct him; instead her dark eyes fixed on his face as if fascinated.

"I've been through a lot," he countered, "and I've been that person, Tobi. My paternity has always been called into question, and though the palace shielded me from it, it came out. Children can be cruel. I couldn't run away from who I was, so I channeled that energy into making a contribution that no one could deny existed. And I'm glad I was successful. I admit, I started it to prove a point. But now I want to be just as successful as king, doing the best for my people—"

He stopped. He hadn't intended to run on for that long, but there was something about having Tobi around that made him want to speak. He cleared his throat. "Well, anyway. That is all."

Something in Tobi's eyes had softened considerably, altering her face completely. It was as if he looked past the woman she presented as on a day-to-day basis, suddenly saw the one she was. He'd seen her sometimes, late at night, nestled into the curve of his arm after a particularly intense session of lovemaking, when they were too tired to hold up those masks they both clung to so desperately. He'd seen glimpses of a future that they might be able to have, if only—

He pushed the thought out of his mind, because his wife had stood and was approaching him, a determined look on her face. She peered down into his, then she smiled.

"I almost believe you mean that," she said, and he laughed and yanked her down onto his lap. The kiss that followed was eager and sloppy, and both were laughing when they separated. Tobi managed to twist just enough to palm his smartphone from the tabletop and shoved it into her shirt.

"Got it," she said triumphantly, and tried to escape, but Akil held her fast.

"You don't want me digging for it," he warned.

"Maybe I do," she shot back—and then gasped when his fingertips gently scissored the nipple that was already swelling for his touch. She was always ready for him, it seemed, and the way those tight buds felt in his *mouth*—

One stroke and it pebbled, and suddenly he was far more interested in that than he was in his phone.

"*No*," she said determinedly, and wriggled off his lap. Her face was alive with laughter, and she backed up. "None of that. Maybe later, if you're as nice to our guests as I want you to be. And I'll hold this till then, too. *No more working.*"

He said she'd make a splendid leader, and frankly, tonight, she felt like the queen she was. *His* queen, no matter how dangerous that was. She stood at the entryway of the Al-Hamri Royal House, welcoming the men and women who were descendants of the oldest houses of Djoboro. She smiled. She laughed. She used the lessons her exasperated stepmother had drilled into her for years to the best effect. She stood, always a half step behind Akil, his hand firmly at her waist. He hadn't let go of her for more than a few minutes the entire evening, and Tobi allowed herself, just for tonight, to imagine they were actual partners, that this was more than a marriage of convenience.

Over the past few weeks her feelings for Akil had blossomed into something else entirely, along with her growing confidence. The mere sight of him sometimes made her body ache.

She felt a hot flush begin at her temples, spread downward. Akil made her aware of her body in ways she didn't know were possible, and she now had to deal with the side effect of wanting him, all the time.

She'd dressed in anticipation of that tonight, in a form-fitting gold gown, and she'd been startled by the woman who looked back at her once she was ready. She looked like the finest ebony dipped in gold. The dress fit so tightly to her curves it was almost indecent, yet covered so much of her skin it was wholly appropriate for that evening. She'd paired the dress with jewels from Akil's family vault—all rubies of course, set in gold so pure it softened from the heat of her skin. For the first time she looked like a woman soft and glowing with affection, wanted and received, not a child longing to escape her loneliness.

Yes. That was it. She wasn't lonely anymore, and Akil was the reason. She dared not articulate what that meant, not with the deal they had on the table, but tonight—

She let him hold her, dance with her, whisper words that dripped with honey. She let him kiss her in dark corners when guests were occupied with revelry, let those long, sensitive fingers tease the skin of her inner thighs till she couldn't take it anymore, laughed low at the dampness he'd created there.

"Later," was all he said, smoothing her skirt down, and, yes, she was thinking about it. She'd progressed to the point where she was fantasizing about them together, new places, new positions, new ways of pleasuring each other. Akil seemed to know her body at this point as much as she did herself.

But they still had a party to get through. And frankly, she thought as she surveyed the gathering with pride, she was becoming as emotionally invested in Djoboro as she was in its king.

I do love it here.

"Wonderful job, my dear," Jamila said to her about halfway through the party. She had spent most of her time sitting on the overstuffed velvet armchair Tobi had prepared for her, and now she patted the arm of it when Tobi came over.

"Are you having fun?" It certainly looked like it to Tobi, and she'd been careful to ensure Jamila was paid the respect she deserved at the dowager princess. Now she gestured that Tobi should bring the plate of delicacies on the table at her elbow a little closer and take some. "I'll wager you haven't eaten all night. Sit for a moment."

"You're right, I've been busy." Tobi laughed, patted her tummy. "This dress doesn't allow for much food, either."

"When you're pregnant it will be important." Jamila looked a little wistful, and Tobi was suddenly overcome. *Children—*

She hadn't allowed herself to think about it, not with her situation being as tenuous as it was. She and Akil used protection. Their marriage was temporary, after all. But she couldn't stop herself imagining that maybe one day a little girl or a little boy, with dark eyes like their father, and her deep skin…

Tobi forced herself back to the present when Jamila spoke. Her eyes looked out over the room with her characteristic sharpness, at the people milling about, talking, laughing, enjoying wine and conversation, illuminated by the gleaming candles and the beauty of the night sky.

"This was a stroke of genius. You are a good partner for him," she said, and smiled at Tobi. "You want what's best for him."

"He wants the same for me," Tobi said, remembering their conversation earlier.

"I'd hope so."

"He's had a rough start to his reign…" Tobi's voice trailed off, just a little. "I hope that this small contribution makes some difference."

"I know. It's a pity it won't."

Tobi blinked. Out of everything that Jamila could have said, she wasn't expecting that. Not at all. "Excuse me?"

"He'll never be the man his father was. Not really." Jamila reached for a whiskey glass and took a long, meditative sip. "I shouldn't tell you, really, but I'm rather tipsy. It'd be nice if someone besides me is there to console him when it doesn't happen."

Tobi's heart was beating so hard she could hear it in her ears, a throb, a rush of blood. She stared at her husband, who was currently laughing with a group of older men. His face was animated. Happier than she'd ever seen it, and she knew it was because he thought, he thought—

"He isn't playing the game, Tobi. His relationship with the old king—he simply doesn't realize how much he was loved and the legacy he built. He's allowed his bitterness to get in the way, and believe me, it is noticed."

Tobi's face must have reflected shock, for Jamila laughed, a little kindly. "You're the daughter of an oba yourself, my dear? Surely you know how old kings are revered?"

"The king is ill!"

"Yes, and his son has exiled him. A pleasant exile, but still an exile. The old king hasn't been seen at a single state ceremony since Malik died, and no one is buying the illness excuse. He attended every single state affair of Malik's, with assistants and nurses, of course. People loved it. Djoboran culture is very much about respect for elders and caring for them. Akil knows this, and he's ignoring the one thing that will never allow people to think he's reformed."

Tobi could not speak, could not answer, only fixed her eyes on Akil, on his happy face. It simply couldn't—

"The old king needs to be at the coronation," Jamila said calmly, downing the last drops of whiskey from her glass. "He needs to be there, or all is lost. You need to make sure of that, or the people won't forget. His father's been hand-training the press for decades, Tobi. They are restrained now out of respect for Malik, but it won't last forever. I don't know how you'll do it, but—trust me, Tobi. I wouldn't steer you wrong."

"You can't tell Akil this yourself?" Tobi felt a sudden rush of anger against Jamila and her ever-smooth, ever-bland, blasé face. But she stood, looking down imperiously at Tobi.

"I'm going to the ladies' lounge," she said. "You stay here and wait for your husband. He will need you in the upcoming days."

With that, she turned and swayed off in the direction of the bathrooms, and Tobi was left with a knot in her stomach bigger than any she'd ever felt before.

CHAPTER FOURTEEN

THE ROYAL CORONATION CEREMONY, the official, public-facing recognition of Akil's accession as king, approached, and Akil found himself descending into razor-sharp focus that manifested in little sleep, little food and hyperconcentration at work. He woke long before the sun was up and slept hours after it set, fortifying himself with coffee as he did so. Tobi's mining apprentice idea had taken on a mind of its own, and had been formally presented to parliament with rousing success. The program would officially be launched in a year's time, and the excitement within the kingdom had become a palpable buzz. The Royal Council had thawed noticeably since the party, and the press had been neutral if not gushing. Finally Djoboro seemed ready for a celebration.

Akil was determined to make a good showing at the ceremony. He was sure he'd terrorized poor Tobi with long detailed descriptions of everything that needed to be done; she was so uncharacteristically quiet and distracted that he finally confronted her a few days before.

"Are you," he said sardonically, "planning to kill me at the forum, like Julius Caesar? I know I've been insufferable for the past few weeks, and you haven't said a word."

"That assumption says more about you than it does about me," Tobi said primly. She was poking at bowl of cream and summer berries with little appetite; Akil's brow furrowed.

"Are you pregnant?" he demanded, and *that* got a reaction from her, at least.

"Heavens, no!"

"Are you on your—"

"If you know what's good for you," she said, eyes flashing dangerously, "you will *not* ask that question."

"Then what's wrong with you?"

"Perhaps it's the fact that I've got such a wonderfully *sensitive* husband," she spat out, but there was an oddness about her expression that made him frown. He tossed his napkin onto the table, leaned in and peered into her face.

"Would you stop?" she exclaimed, drawing back.

He knew he was irritating her, but he had to get some reaction out of her. "Are you nervous about the coronation?"

"What is this, twenty questions?"

"I'm not sure what you're referring to."

"It's an expression. This game—" Seeing his face, she gave up. "Why do you care, anyway? It's not like I'm here because my feelings matter."

Akil heaved a sigh. "If by this point, Tobi, you think I don't care about your feelings, you are more disillusioned than you let on."

At that, something in his wife's face tightened; then she looked down at her hands. He waited, taking a sip of the rich Turkish coffee, savoring the bitter taste.

"I don't know what I'm supposed to do after this is all over," she said, gesturing vaguely at the gorgeous sprawl of land that lay before them, bathed in the pale light of the early morning. "I mean, what? Go back to Dubai? Nigeria?"

"You have something to do in Dubai, if I recall, and you will have the full support of the palace behind you." He had to kill this now, before emotion turned it into something unpleasant, something he did not want to deal with at the moment. "Tobi, you can do anything you want to do! Finish your women's housing project, get firmly entrenched in philanthropy. An economics degree. Documentaries, if you're determined to do film. I can set you up on a goodwill tour, and you can talk about the mining program. It was your brainchild, after all, and I've given you full credit. The role of working royal is yours."

"Just not the role of your wife," she said softly.

Did she want that? He dared not ask. "I'm not asking you for a divorce, Tobi, although you certainly can have one, if you want one."

"You'd be surprised," Tobi muttered, pushing back the offending bowl. A server appeared, took it away.

"I can't promise to love you, Tobi. We set this deal in place so we could both walk away."

"And what if I don't want to?"

The silence in the room was so loud it was practically echoing, and Akil felt a sudden rush of half defensiveness, half anger. So she would force his hand, then?

"Tobi, you have to," he said, and his voice held a note of pleading in it.

"Have to…what? Completely ignore the fact that every time I'm in your bed it hurts a little more because I know I must remember it can't mean anything? Ignore the fact that I have my own projects here now, my own responsibilities—do you intend that I walk away from them? I'm *human*, Akil. And so are you. If you want an adviser, you've plenty of those. I'm your queen. And I want to at least explore the possibility of being that in every sense. I mean we already are, aren't we? You just refuse to acknowledge it, and for someone who prides himself on plain speaking—" She broke off at last and half turned, presumably to hide her face.

Her outburst left Akil's skin tingling and an odd stinging behind his eyes.

"Do you want to stay?" he asked after a moment, taking a breath to ensure his voice would be steady. "Here?"

"Am I allowed to want that?" Her voice sounded choked.

That blossoming warmth that belonged to her, that lived deep in his chest, was sparking at the sound of her words. It was as if she were offering him something cool to drink, something to relieve a thirst he hadn't known he had until it was there, spilling over the edges of her hands.

He'd married Tobi to fill a need he'd had at the time. Now she seemed the answer to other needs he'd allowed to go dormant for a very long time. The most frightening thing was that he could so easily picture what their lives together would look like, and her place in it. It happened every time she sat across from him to have a meal, or spoke with him about matters of state, or drew her scented softness close in their clean white bed.

Her large dark eyes were fixed on his face

now, and she'd crept forward, just a little. "Akil…" she whispered.

"Beautiful Tobi," he said quietly, and then followed up with words in his language. They were low and soft and altogether too quickly said for Tobi to even begin to understand them, but the unexpected tenderness behind them was real, and when his lips met hers neither was surprised.

"Akil," Tobi murmured. It felt somehow as if they were breaking a rule, and she wasn't sure whether she should be the one to acknowledge it, or her husband should. All she knew was that if he continued to kiss her like this and then pull away, she would be left feeling so much colder, and so much emptier, than she had before.

"Be quiet," he said in what was perhaps the gentlest voice she'd ever heard from him, and cradled her face in his hands.

This was disconcerting for more reasons than the obvious. Tobi felt desire, but it was nothing like the heady indefinable lust that usually characterized their encounters. This was want, but a want for tenderness. She wanted to be held. She wanted to be cradled in the shelter of his arms, the way he was doing now.

She wanted to be close to Akil. And for just a few seconds, physically at least, he was letting her in. And it felt better than anything else she'd ever experienced.

She should just stop him. She should make a sarcastic comment, or a joke, or brace her hands against that massive chest and push back, push away from the hurt that was sure to come if she stayed here. But she did not. She stepped into the circle of his arms, tucked her head with a sigh and allowed Akil to continue kissing her.

"Please, please—" she whispered, bringing his hands up to palm her breasts, arching against him with a deep-rooted need that there was no point in suppressing. She was surprised when her husband's self-control shattered as quickly as hers. In moments her skirt had been hiked up to her thighs, and before she could scream, before the shudders that tightened her body completed, he was between her legs and finally, *finally* inside her.

He was speaking words against her ear. Rasping out things that made her shake. *I need you, I need you now, just like this—*

This was madness, she thought hazily before everything shattered into a million bursts of color and light and she became a trembling, panting facsimile of herself. They did not speak, only clung wordlessly to each other, having used each other for something absolutely vital.

"Are you all right?" he asked, and when she

nodded, he kissed her, closed-mouthed. He looked calmer now, too, she noted as she slid from beneath him, ignoring the wetness between her thighs.

She couldn't stop trembling. Despite the raw, disjointed nature of their union today, it'd been their most intimate yet.

I need you. No, *I need you* now. She'd never forget those words, breathed hotly against the shell of her ear, or the shakiness of his voice as he'd said them. Akil, who'd never needed anyone in his life, had admitted he did. To her. There were marks on her body that were proof of his urgent passion, but they were nothing compared to the marks left on her heart.

She loved him. She loved her tempestuous, arrogant, passionate husband with all her heart. She'd fallen in love with his strength, his dedication, his commitment to the country he loved. He'd humbled her, possessed her, and she reveled in it.

Tobi headed to her PR committee meeting that afternoon feeling as if she were floating, still feeling Akil's lips on hers, his gentle hands warm and sure on her body. He hadn't pushed her away for the first time. He'd drawn her into the circle of his arms instead, reluctant as it might have been. And for the first time, she had a name for the feelings she'd been trying to fight for weeks.

Not love—she could not presume to think of that, now. But she was beginning to know what she wanted, and where Akil fit in that. And for the first time, those small daydreams seemed tinged with possibility. It was quite a trip back to earth, hearing David's dry voice bringing up his pet subject: Akil's relationship with his father.

"We believe the king should be a part of the coronation ceremony," he told her. "In some way, at least." The execution would be fairly simple. The old king was to watch the coronation ceremony from a secured location, and was to be brought out—briefly—on a balcony to wave to the people, shortly after his son was crowned. He would be flanked by Jamila and Tobi, who would ensure he was whisked away as quickly as he was seen.

"It's the only way," David said crisply. "Remember, Tobi. This is for his good, about creating a narrative. He'll never have to appear in public again after this, if we want."

We're manipulating an old, sick man, Tobi thought, but goodness knew that the former king would probably approve of such manipulations himself, were he lucid enough to hear the plan. However, she wasn't worried about the old king; she was worried about Akil.

"There's no way the king will agree," she said simply. "It's a good idea, but you must find another way."

"This is the best way." David leaned forward, eyes gleaming with conviction. "It will allow the people to see that he doesn't shun tradition, whatever his personal feelings. And he doesn't have to know, Your Majesty. A single moment, and it'll be over. He won't be able to do anything about it after it's done, and he's given you leave to approve every PR move."

She could still taste the spice of him on her lips, and the sensation was made uncomfortable by David's suggestion. "I couldn't not tell him—"

"Surely you see the importance of this," he pressed.

She did. The worst part was that she did. Being a monarch was being slave to tradition; she was part of a royal house herself. But there was something that sparked so new, so vital in Akil that she'd been attracted to since the beginning.

Would it really be folly to support him in finding his own way instead? Was there a medium? A compromise?

What had her husband said about David's

team? *They overstep their bounds.* Still, he'd hired them for a reason, hadn't he? And were she being completely honest, Tobi saw nothing but sense in the team's suggestion. She hated the fact that all the good her husband had done in the past few weeks had been brushed away by the sting of public perception.

If she did this, she knew it wasn't just about his father—it was about opposing Akil, for the supposed good of the country. And in light of the encounter they'd just had…she shifted, feeling her body grow ever more tense.

CHAPTER FIFTEEN

HE'D ANSWERED THE question completely wrong, Akil thought, closing his eyes against the memory of that morning with his wife. She'd asked him—outright—if she could stay. And instead of drawing back, of putting up that wall that would keep her at a safe distance from the damaged man he was—he'd drawn her in instead. Kissed her. Touched her. Caressed her. Reveled in the soft warmth of a body that was beginning to feel like…home.

He hadn't had time to panic then, with her nestled in his arms. Now he was. This was not going to plan, not at all, and he didn't know what to do about it.

What do you want, Akil? Would it really be so difficult to let her in? To allow the possibility of something different—something lasting—to take the place of his grand plan?

Akil pushed back from the massive desk in the king's study, stood to his feet and began to pace, as he was wont to do when in deep thought. His reasons for keeping Tobi at arm's length felt flimsier with each encounter, with each kiss.

He was a man who prided himself on honesty. But the thought of facing the truth about Tobi? His stomach knotted so tightly he had to pause for a moment and draw a deep breath.

He started at the soft knock on his door, and at his "Come in!" Tobi appeared, holding a manila folder against her chest. She was clearly coming from a meeting; her braids were twisted into a high knot, and she wore a pencil skirt and button-down. Even in this simple dress and minimal makeup she looked stunning—as much as she did on his arm, in their throne room, in his bed...

Heat suffused his body from head to toe. Was he smitten to the point of ridiculousness, then? His father had been much the same way, and look at what happened to *him*.

Akil cleared his throat.

"Hello," she said in a voice that was quiet, almost deferential. "May I speak to you?"

"Of course." He gestured for her to sit and she did so, crossing her legs. His eyes flickered over the smooth dark expanse of thigh she revealed before he forced his eyes back to her face.

What the hell was he, a teenager? No. He'd never been this ridiculous as a teenager.

Tobi was speaking now, fiddling with the manila envelope as if she were trying to decide whether to speak or not. "Can I ask you something?"

"I don't know, can you?" he said drily.

She ignored the sarcasm and forged ahead. "Why—" She bit her lip. "I never got an answer to what I asked last night. Why don't you want me to stay?"

The air seemed to still as the words hung between them, and Tobi continued.

"Making love to me—it isn't an answer really. You—we've never had any trouble connecting in bed. And we can't—we have to be honest with ourselves, Akil. There's something."

She was right, and the sincerity of the words were blocking his own from coming out. He set his jaw and looked out toward the wide window, the rugs, the bookshelves—anywhere but at the woman in front of him.

"I'm not expecting some huge declaration, Akil. That'd be stupid. But I do have feelings for you. I won't admit more than that, but they're there. And more than that, I love it here. It's beginning to feel like home. And If I'm expected to go—"

"Tobi—"

"It's better sooner rather than later. Before this gets any deeper," she said simply.

Akil closed his eyes briefly, then stood and crossed the room to an upholstered two-seater in place for visitors. What he had to say couldn't be done across a massive desk, and he wanted to give her that respect at least. "Will you sit with me?"

She assented, and when the two were settled he began to talk, looking down at his hands the entire time.

"My mother," he said, "was young when she married my father, and quite in love with him. I think she resented his dedication to his rule, to his public service and, well, she felt neglected, and she acted out. There was an affair. There were affairs," he corrected, and his mouth was tight.

Tobi let out a breath slowly. "Oh."

"I was born in the midst of all this. You can imagine the drama," he said crisply. "I am my father's son, of course, he verified that years ago, but the effects of his wife's betrayal stayed with him. I think a part of him still believed, despite all the evidence, that I might not be his son, or worse yet, that I was a son conceived out of duty, not loyalty or affection. He drank a great deal. It didn't affect his rule, he was clever enough not to let it, but it was *not* a happy upbringing for me, Tobi. And I rebelled because of it. I can't—I watched that turn my father into what he was—"

Tobi's eyes were glimmering with unshed tears. "Do you think me capable of that sort of betrayal then?"

Akil shook his head so vigorously it seemed in danger of leaving his shoulders. "No—*never.* I don't trust *myself* not to turn into him. I'm completely unequipped to love, Tobi, the way that you deserve. And I believe that to try it— it'd be a costly experiment, Tobi. There's no guarantee—"

She could barely hear what he was saying; there was roaring in her ears. She'd poured her heart out only for him to say this?

"You don't get into a relationship because it's *guaranteed,* Akil!" She had to take a breath before continuing. "I actually feel sorry for you." Her chin was trembling now; she could not stop it even if she wanted to. "You think so little of yourself, when the truth is that you have everything. It's a sad place to be."

"You presume too much," Akil said through his teeth.

"You're one of Africa's top economists. You're rich as Midas." She began ticking off on her fingers. "You literally have the opportunity to change the entire financial outlook of your country, and you have such a capacity for kindness." Her voice broke a little on the last word. "I saw it in so many forms that I almost fell in love with you. And even with all that, you choose instead to cling to the unwanted bastard prince that he made you into—"

"You go too far!" His face was dark with anger and she was glad!

She'd finally, finally broken through the facade, and Akil lunged to his feet. The sudden movement made him throw out an arm for balance, and Tobi automatically ducked, throwing her own arms up to protect her head. A moment later she lowered them to see her husband's horrified face.

"Tobi. I wasn't going to hit you!"

"I know. I—" Tobi began backing up. Akil was still speaking, but she couldn't hear him; there was a rushing in her ears, all humiliation and sadness and finally, an acceptance that this had to end. She turned on her heel and ran. Ran from the confrontation, ran from the mingled shock and anger and regret on his face, ran from everything. It would not take long to pack. She'd never wanted to be back in her old wardrobe more than she did now.

True to form, she stumbled before making it over the threshold and Akil was there, steading her, big hands on her shoulders. She swore and turned, shoving him with all her might.

"Leave me alone!"

"I will not." His voice was low and urgent. "Tobi—I wasn't going to strike you. I would never. Especially not after the way I grew up—"

Tears were falling hard and fast now, and she no longer tried to stop them. "I don't want to talk about this anymore."

"Tobi—"

"No," she said forcefully. "I initially came to talk to you about the coronation. David wanted us to bring your father out, to have him as part of the ceremony, all without telling you. I told them off, Akil. I told them that you'd always been your own person, your own king, and they should give you the respect and the courtesy to win over your people as yourself. I told them that I trusted you, and if they didn't have the wherewithal to find a solution, they weren't the team for you. I believe in you—I believe in what you're doing. But I won't let it extend to this— I simply won't."

She finished her speech and stood, chest heaving, face tense and drawn. When Akil reached for her she shook her head violently, stepped back.

"I'm going to leave," she choked out. "I'm going back to Dubai. Oh—don't worry, I'll be back for the ceremony, and all the state events. But if this is how you want it, I'm not going to wait for you to throw me out."

"Tobi—"

"I'm not going to go any deeper, Akil—it hurts far too much."

He let her go. He let her stumble to the bed-chamber they shared, let her throw clothing in a bag, let her charter the Royal Flyer to head back to Dubai. He didn't stop any of it.

The night that Tobi left, Akil did not go home. Tobi would not be there, filling the hallways with her spirit and laughter. Despite his best efforts, Akil could not banish the image of his wife standing before him, tears running down her face, and then, worst of all, cowering as he shouted like he was a—

Akil shook his head to clear it. If he were really serious about intending to cut Tobi from his life, he couldn't think about any of this; there could be no regrets, no hesitation. He could not think about the fact that his wife, despite his best efforts, had forced out his own secrets— and the two had more in common than he ever could have imagined. Akil had rarely been in the position of caring about someone other than himself, and he found the prospect no more than a little terrifying especially—

His heart was involved. That much was clear; he wasn't that self-delusional. But what was he going to do about it?

Akil prepared for bed that night, stripping down to his undershirt and neatly folding his trousers at the foot of the sofa in his office. His secretary would not blink an eye when she came in the next morning; she was used to the eccentricities of her employer, and Akil often stayed the night when he was working on a particularly complicated problem. This problem had nothing to do with economics or the state of the nation, however. It had everything to do with his heart, and with Tobi's.

He did not love her—he could not love her! But as the hours ticked by with no promise of sleep, he could not deny that he was here, wondering how she was, barely able to hold himself back from texting her, from begging for her forgiveness. He'd treated her with such a callous lack of consideration, and he knew, deep down, that he was completely in the wrong.

She had not acknowledged the money he'd wired to her as soon as his staff confirmed she was off the premises, but she hadn't sent it back, either. Hopefully the realities of life outside the palace would make her do exactly what he wished: take the money, go away. His guilt kept reconstructing the crumpled figure of his wife as she ran from him hours before, but he whispered back reassuring truths to himself. Tobi was young. She was beautiful. She would eventually find something to do, find another person to love, and she would be absolutely fine.

The thought of her being with anybody but him made his stomach clench so tightly he attempted to get up and run for the restroom, then forced himself to stay exactly where he was. This lurch of his insides was guilt. It had completely crippled him, and he knew he was entirely in the wrong.

So what the hell was he to do, then? What was next?

Akil had never in his life been without a plan, had never been in a place where he wasn't sure what happened next. He lay on his back, stared up at the ceiling of his office and wondered exactly how it had gotten to this point.

Never in all his years had Prince Akil Al-Hamri felt regret, but he did now. It didn't matter, the fact that he'd cleared all physical evidence of her.

She still haunted the corridors in his memory, and those came hard and fast: their white-hot arguments and passionate reconciliations. The way she smelled, all spice and sun. The tangy sweet taste of her skin. The way her smile brightened up her face, and the way she listened to him. Engaged with him.

He hadn't known he was lonely until she left.

Whenever his chest tightened with what felt uncomfortably like regret, he listed the benefits of her leaving, mentally. He'd married Tobi for her royal status, nothing else. His near-violent attraction to her had startled him, but he hadn't let it get in the way of his faculties. He would not love her; he could not love her. His focus had to be on the throne; he had no room for anything else. A woman would have been a distraction, a diversion away from the plans he had.

What he hadn't expected was that Tobi would have proven herself an equal partner in all this, a force of her own to be reckoned with. He also hadn't expected—

No.

If he let his thoughts run on, who knew where they would end up? He'd made his decision; Tobi was gone. He was alone again. He would go off, find a quiet place to lick his wounds, regroup, return, figure out what to do with the rest of his life.

He was king, and finally—reluctantly, but finally—his people were beginning to accept him as such.

So, what now?

When Akil finally exited the palace, the sun

had long sunk in the sky, and a glance at his watch told him it was well after nine thirty. Good. Everyone would be asleep. He wouldn't even be going back to the house were it not for some legal documents he needed; he hated the sight of the place now.

When his driver silently opened the back door of the massive SUV that waited in the parking lot, Akil peered into it, then looked at his driver.

"You're fired," he said with excruciating calm.

"No, he's not. He's been in the family's employ since before you could drive. Get in, Akil. And Elias, be so good as to take a turn around the parking lot. We should be done in ten minutes or so."

The driver disappeared, and Akil set his jaw. It was the last person he expected to see. In the wan light of the back of the car, Jamila looked very tired.

"I cannot believe you made me chase you," she said.

"What do you want?"

She sighed. "I want you to know how very disappointed in you I am, Akil."

Disappointed! "I dare say—"

"You don't. And you won't. This is my piece. What I'm talking about is the abominable way you've treated your wife. Your *wife,* Akil."

She stopped talking for a moment, took in a heavy breath. "That girl is in *love* with you, and you allowed it. You took her into your bed— yes, it's obvious by the way she looked at you, don't deny it—and made her think of herself as a valuable part of your life, and then cast her aside. It's actually more despicable than anything your father ever did. He was disgraceful, but his wife? Her feet didn't touch the ground, and he didn't care who knew it."

"We had a deal," Akil ground out.

"That you bullied her into. And then she unfortunately fell in love with you." She shook her head hard. "I'm a widow, Akil, before my time. Malik regretted the breakdown of your relationship so much. He tried his best as a child to make sure you felt loved. But I fear it broke something elemental in you instead. You need to examine yourself. Return to your wife. Divorce her properly if that's what you both want, but this—straddling two lives—this isn't fair, Akil. To either of you."

The two stared at each other for a long moment; then, Jamila sighed, her face returning to its usual inscrutability.

"There's Elias, trying to be discreet," she said, and waved his driver back over. "Drop me off at my own house, Akil. I've said all I wanted to say."

Akil swallowed hard, then waved a hand to Elias in assent. When Jamila was safely back at her home, he sagged back against the leather cushions of the car.

You made her think of herself as a valuable part of your life, and then cast her aside.

He did not want to remember Jamila's words, but the memory of Tobi's stricken face stopped him cold. He hadn't intended to do it. Tobi's sweet stubbornness had crept through his defenses with a strength that had been surprising to both of them. He'd taken advantage of her innocence, whispered sweet words in their intimate moments, gained her trust. The fact that he'd intended no malice mattered little; he'd carry the shattered look on her face with him for a very long time, if not forever.

And she was still his wife.

Somewhere, beneath all the callousness and jadedness beat the heart of a man with a conscience. And in that heart, he knew he'd done her wrong.

He also knew he loved her, beyond anything he thought himself capable of. The seeds had been planted the night of their wedding, when he looked into the eyes of the frightened girl who held herself erect despite her union with a perfect stranger. He'd admired her. Three years later, he'd desired her, possessed her. And now…

This isn't fair...to either of you.

Jamila was right. And he burned with something he could not quite yet name.

Shame, perhaps.

Arriving at the Dubai International Airport felt in some ways like stepping back through a portal in one of those children's fairy tales after the heroine has been asleep. Time seemed to have stood still in some ways. Arrivals was still swarming with tourists, students on break, visitors from every country imaginable and wealthy housewives in fluttery black abayas with their white-robed husbands steering them gently forward, hounding groups of chubby-cheeked children in voices tired from hours of flight. There were women like her, young, spectacularly dressed, fully made up, looking for love and adventure in the desert heat. Tobi felt as if she had been transported to the past, a past where she didn't belong anymore. She realized she belonged in Djoboro, in the ruby-studded house with the windows facing the sea, pressed close in the embrace of a man who even now, in the depths of her hurt, made her heart tighten with longing until the point of pain.

Before she hit the baggage claim, she received an alert that her account had been credited. It was a huge amount and that made Tobi even angrier, a hollow sort of anger that was tempered with self-disgust. A message followed:

We don't have to talk about this now, Tobi. But I'll be in touch.

She'd brought this on herself, selling herself to a man with no human feeling. Tobi wished more than anything that she could return the money immediately, but she was about to head into the great unknown, without any idea where she was going.

She still had the numbers of the producers she was speaking to before Akil had reappeared in her life, but she'd ghosted them for weeks, with no intention of ever going back. She simply wasn't for that world anymore, but what was she supposed to do now? She had truly put her life on hold for a man who had set her aside without a thought. How could anyone possibly be so cold?

And yet she knew she could not have imagined the moments they'd spent together, the intensity of his gaze, the gentleness of his touch, the way he'd considered her, listened to her, held what she said in high regard. Akil didn't hate her, and part of Tobi wondered whether hatred might have been easier. He'd liked her. He respected her but had chosen, once presented with her heart, not to love her.

That rejection hurt more than anything else.

Tobi ignored the fragrant stalls advertising duty-free perfume, chocolates and other delicacies, and instead went directly to a taxicab, taking it to the Chantilly Hotel and asking for a quiet room overlooking the marina. She threw open her suitcase and took a look, then had to blink. The bright, colorful clothing assaulted her eyes for the first few moments. After the life of quiet opulence she'd lived for the past few months, her old garments looked overblown, garish.

Who was she anymore? It was as if the stubborn, strong-minded girl she'd been had transformed into something else under Akil's overbearing hand—but it'd been more than that. Her father had tried to bully her into being something she wasn't, and she'd never capitulated. Even with all his nonsense, Akil had done more than that—he'd shown her new sides of herself, and she'd blossomed under his tutelage as well as his touch, sexually as well as intellectually. He'd shown her possibilities for her own life that she'd never had before.

He'd made her truly feel like she had the ability to be a person of significance, for the first time in her life. And even in her anger, in her grief, she lifted her chin, set her jaw. It didn't have to stop here. She'd had a vision, hadn't she? She wanted to make the world a little bit more hospitable to girls and women who had no other options. She would take the money Akil had sent, and she would *make* it happen!

Broken heart or not.

I'm going to have a shower, get dressed and think this through. Tobi leaped into the enormous marble-tiled shower in her suite, allowing water as hot as she could stand it to beat down on her body until she couldn't tell where her skin began and the stream of water ended. She used the rosewater-scented body wash liberally and stepped out, dripping, on the mat. She rubbed herself briskly, anointed herself with lavender oil, shea butter, and sprayed perfume until the clouds of it made her cough. Then she donned the skimpiest, brightest thing she could find in the wardrobe—a sparkly mini-dress of marigold yellow—did her makeup, ran her fingers through the tiny braids she'd taken to wearing in Djoboro, and surveyed herself in the mirror.

The girl staring back at her looked like Tobi, perhaps except for the eyes. Those were sunken and sad, but they were also brighter. Wiser.

In some ways, she'd found herself in Djoboro. She'd gained faith in her own abilities.

She'd, for the first time, been taken seriously when she came up with an idea, and her husband had treated her with the same consideration as he would any other adviser. The girl Tobi had caught a glimpse of the woman, the queen she might become, and leaving that so quickly was something that weighed heavy on her heart.

But she was still Tobi, wasn't she? She could make this happen anywhere.

She glanced down at her phone. No texts, no calls from Akil. He hadn't even checked in to see that she'd arrived safely, although she knew that his many representatives around the hotel would get that news back to him quickly. And for now, despite her grand revelations, she'd never felt more alone in her life. She navigated to her contacts, scrolled down and called a familiar number.

Her sister picked up on the first ring.

"You are in Dubai," Kemi said, and her gentle voice made tears spring to Tobi's eyes. She blinked them back, hard; she didn't want to cry anymore.

"How on earth did you know?" Tobi sank down into one of the plush armchairs at the window that faced the sea. She could see boats on the water, little dots of gray and white on brilliant blue, while the Dubai skyline loomed over the marina in sharp relief. It was beautiful, everything that she wanted, but something deep inside her longed for the gentle slopes and brilliant green of Djoboro's landscape. She craved the country she'd grown to love, just as much as the man she'd left behind there.

"Akil called me," Kemi said, "and told me to expect your call." There was a pause, and her sister chuckled, a low sound that reverberated over the line. "I'm downstairs."

"You're what?" Tobi sprang to her feet and ran to the door, throwing it open as if her sister could materialize just by her doing that.

"Yes, I flew over as soon as Akil told me." Her sister paused. "Are you all right, little sister?"

Tobi took a great gasp of air that was both laughter and crying at the same time. "I don't know whether to be thrilled or horrified that you're here. I'm such a mess, Kemi. It all is such a *mess.*"

"Come downstairs then, and we'll talk."

Tobi was already flying toward the elevators. When she reached the bottom floor, she saw Kemi immediately, looking as round and comforting as she had months ago, when she'd last seen her. Her face and body were still soft with her recent birth, and her eyes, though heavy with lack of sleep, were the happiest Tobi had ever seen them. She rushed straight into Kemi's arms and closed her eyes, allowing herself to be engulfed with the familiar, subtly sweet scent of lilies of the valley.

"Oh, my love, you've been crying," Kemi said softly, and rubbed her sister's back in gentle circles. Tobi didn't even bother denying it.

"I think I might be able to stop, now that you're here," she said in a voice that quavered a bit. She pulled back and kissed her older sister on both cheeks. "You look well," she said, and sniffed. "I hope Luke doesn't hate me for dragging you out here and dumping him with the children."

"Please don't give that man any sympathy," said Kemi. "He's being backed up by an army of nannies and staff, and he has a set schedule for the twins every single day until I'm back."

"Sounds very much like Luke." Tobi laughed a little shakily. Her sister reached out and placed gentle fingers under her chin, raising it up so that she could read her face. "You look sad around the eyes," Kemi said. "But otherwise, you look well. It looks as if he was able to get you to hold still long enough to put on a little weight." She tilted her head, considering more. "No, actually, it isn't weight at all. You look softer. More womanly."

Tobi felt her face get hot; she knew exactly

what it was. It was something that she noticed when she looked in the mirror herself, the fact that she was now soft and radiant with tenderness given and received. During her weeks with Akil, something blossomed, something that had taken the girl that she was, turned her into a woman who *needed*.

"How long can you stay?" she whispered.

Her sister's face grew grave. "As long as you want me to. But I'm hoping that you won't need me, because he'll come and get you."

If only. She closed her mouth against a laugh.

The whole story came out, little by little, amid plates of shawarma and hummus and fried chicken, enjoyed in the privacy of a curtained booth in the hotel restaurant. After, they retreated to Kemi's big airy suite, switched on the television to watch Turkish dramas and leaned on each other on the big bed, much as they used to do years ago, while in their father's house. After speaking at length about Akil, Kemi talked a little about her own marriage, something that Tobi appreciated. It was not in her nature to brood over anything for a considerable amount of time, and she was already tired of crying, although there was a hollowness at her core that she felt nothing would ever fill.

"Don't be afraid of loving him, no matter how much it hurts," Kemi said softly. It was two in the morning, and they sat among the greasy wrappers from their dinner and late-night snacks. Tobi could not sleep and Kemi wouldn't, so her older sister had begun re-braiding her hair for her, using a small container of gel to smooth the soft wooliness of her hair into neat cornrows that framed her face. "It's your right, Tobi. Never feel bad for having feelings for anyone. It shows that you're open to love, even if he's not, and there's nothing wrong with that. Akil—" She took a breath. "Love scares him. But when love blossoms, and is given space to grow, it expands inside you until it pushes out all the fear. It fills your heart until there's no room for anything else, and it's special. It makes us human."

Tobi closed her eyes, listening to her sister's musical voice, ringing with the tenderness that comes from loving and having been loved. She knew that Kemi was right. She also knew that the most painful part of this, and what Kemi hadn't addressed yet, was that it would be Akil's decision, and his alone, when it came to loving her back.

He's already made his decision, hasn't he?

Quietly, head resting deep in the recesses of her sister's soft lap, Tobi reached into her heart, let go of Akil.

If loving him was at the cost of her own self-respect, her own self-worth—

Don't do it. She had to be a queen unto her own self, regardless of what her title was in person.

If Akil was lost to her; she had to move on.

CHAPTER SIXTEEN

ONLY A YEAR AGO, Tobi would've been absolutely delighted to be walking down the hall of the Chantilly Hotel in the company of Samuel Ojo, one of the biggest philanthropists in Ogun State, whom she'd pitched her idea to for the Obatola Safe House for Girls and Women two weeks ago, with her full royal titles signed proudly at the bottom. She'd done her research this time, hiring planners from David Ashton's firm to run the entire project. After days spent brooding, crying, feeling sad and, quite frankly, waiting for Akil to call, Tobi had finally given up and made a few calls of her own.

"I'm thrilled you find this a promising opportunity," she said, shaking the older man's hand smoothly, and walked him down the hall to the main conference room, where her planning team awaited to pitch what she'd worked on night and day. "I'm so keen to work with you."

"I should be saying that to you," the older

man said, and smiled. "It's a wonderful initiative, Your Majesty, and much needed."

"It's one very close to my heart." Tobi pushed open the door to the massive conference room, and she blinked and took it in. Sunlight streamed from skylights up above, and the room was decorated with the same sort of opulent style that was so characteristic of this part of the world. The floor was carpeted in cerulean blue and gold, and the massive wood conference table was flanked by luxuriously soft padded chairs. However, none of this registered to Tobi, for her entire planning team was gone, and the lone man seated at the table was none other than—

"So you were the one who's had David's attention divided this entire time," Akil said in his usual soft, accented voice. "I had a hell of a time getting the name of his new client out of him." His eyes fixed on her, her face, her hot-pink manicure, matching skirt and blouse, and the distinguished businessman at her side. Tobi stood frozen, then found her tongue with some effort.

"I've got a presentation right now," she said woodenly.

Samuel's eyes darted between Tobi and Akil. "This is—"

"Her husband, Akil Al-Hamri, king of Djoboro," Akil said smoothly. "Mr. Ojo—sorry,

I read the name on the presentation folders—
might I borrow my wife for a few moments? A
bit of an emergency has come up."

"Why, of course." Samuel cleared his throat
and turned to her. "Your Majesty."

"Tobi, please," she managed to say through
lips that felt frozen. "And really, Mr. Ojo, there
is no need—"

"There's no trouble at all. You've very generously booked me till tomorrow, and I'm happy
to have a drink. Just call up when you're ready."
He said farewell to them both and was gone,
leaving Tobi breathing hard, staring at Akil in
a mixture of shock and fury.

"I'm sorry for crashing, but you've kept your
movements very covered," Akil said simply. His
dark eyes rested on her face with an intensity
that froze her inside. "You see, Tobi, I found it
quite impossible to get on without you."

She stood very, very still and concentrated all
her efforts on breathing in and out. Akil's mouth
tipped. He eased out from the conference table
and walked over to her, his hands pushed deep
in the pockets of the linen trousers he wore.

"Well?" he asked mildly.

Tobi blinked hard, then turned and walked away
as rapidly as she could in her high heels. She
had no thought except to get away from him,

and *now*. Akil's footsteps quickened behind her, and she began to run. It was futile; Akil's hand was at her elbow, and she found herself hustled into a family restroom. Akil closed the door and locked it.

He looked down at Tobi, who was still gaping at him.

"Are you *crazy*?"

"You're beautiful when you're angry," he rasped with a heat in his eyes that made the blood rush to her face. He reached down to touch her chin, but she yanked back.

"Don't touch me. *Don't touch me!*"

"Tobi—"

To her horror, she started to cry, and it wasn't just a few tears, either. It was ugly and loud and wrenching, the culmination of everything that had been building between them for ages. He reached out presumably to calm her, but she shrank away from him.

"I hate you," she said emphatically, and pressed her palms to her eyes. She could not look at him, at that grave expression. She heard him clear his throat, and felt him press a square of clean white fabric into her hands. She took it, mopped blindly at her face.

"I'm sorry I did that, but it was the only way I could think of to get your attention," he said after a moment as Tobi struggled for breath. She had to regain her dignity. She *had* to.

"You couldn't have called? Sent a message?"

"Would you have replied? I wouldn't have."

"Leave," Tobi ordered, her voice shaking. Akil was all she could see, filling the frame of her vision, all broad shoulders and dark eyes, eyes that spoke far too much. She backed up until she couldn't, until the back of her legs touched one of the large soft armchairs in the lounge area, and she sank into the seat. Her heart was hammering so hard she imagined most of the blood in her body had rerouted there, leaving her very light-headed. Akil looked down at her for a long moment, then sank down so quickly Tobi gasped aloud, and rested his dark head in her lap.

"Oluwatobilola," he said, and her full name never sounded quite as sweet as it did now, rumbling low from his chest. "Tobi. Please. My love, please—"

He was saying words that didn't quite make sense, because she was swallowing hard, trying desperately to keep from crying. Her fingers slid as if on instinct to the dark curls clustered on his head; the smell and feel of him was overwhelming. Her body contracted, softened for him almost involuntarily. It completely ignored her reasoning, her anger, her resentment. It was as if her body was determined to conform to the shape of him, yield to the hands gripping her thighs, surrender completely to his will without her permission. They were not in bed, they were fully clothed, but yearning knifed through her as if they'd never been separated. He did not speak, but the message in his stance was clear.

An entire king, at *her* feet.

"No," she said, but her voice was feeble, and Akil raised his head. A gentle smile lifted the corner of his mouth, and Tobi's heart skipped a beat, even as she grasped mentally for strength. She found some in the anger that had resided low in her gut since she'd left Djoboro.

She struggled to her feet, and in a flash Akil stood, too.

"What the hell are you doing here?" she demanded, and was distressed to hear that her voice did sound exactly as she felt, exhilarated as well as afraid. She was trembling like the limbs of the iroko tree during Harmattan, and allowing Akil to cup her cheek in his hand, to look deep in her eyes.

"Tobi," he said again, his voice tender. "Please—"

That was the last thing she understood completely, for he began speaking in a mix of Djoboran and English, as if the latter was inadequate to express the depth of his feelings. What he said was so accented and so rough she could not catch most of it, but the meaning was clear.

He was begging. For her pardon, for her forgiveness.

She stopped him by bracing a hand on his chest; that was a mistake. She could feel muscle working under the thin fabric of his shirt, and he trapped her hand there with his before she could step sideways, make her escape.

"Tobi?"

She swallowed hard. "You know I didn't understand anything you said."

At that, his lips quirked up, ever so slightly. "I said that I'm sorry," he replied simply. The raw emotion of minutes before was gone, and in its place a steadiness that was no less terrifying in its intensity. "I came to beg your forgiveness. And to come for my wife, if she will have me."

Tobi was appalled at how her heart leaped at those few words; was she really so much a fool, after all? "You didn't want me," she whispered.

Akil's face was grave, but it still had so much tenderness in it that her heart constricted despite herself. "Yes," he agreed.

"Give me one good reason why I should just…" Her voice trailed off, and Akil's heavy brows drew together. He straightened to his full height, and once again, Tobi felt the space grow smaller, as if he were filling the room with his essence. The difference now, though, was that hers seemed to meld with his. He was drawing her in, or trying to. He wasn't crowding her out.

"You shouldn't," he said simply. "I don't know if I would. But I was wrong, Tobi. And I am here to say that without reservation, whether the story ends in my favor or not."

Tobi's heart was drumming in her ears; she closed her eyes for a brief moment.

"Have you ever thought of what we could be, *habibti?*" he said, and the tenderness in his voice cramped low in her stomach. She folded her arms protectively round herself, but he was closing in on her; she could feel his warmth on her skin, smell salt and starch and sandalwood and everything that was undoubtedly Akil.

Had she thought of what they could be? Of course she had.

"We had potential. So much potential. And I failed to see it." The warmth of his lips were a fraction of an inch away from her temple; he would take her in his arms next, she knew, and if he did that all would be lost. She'd no longer hold the cards. Her cursed attraction to Akil was a weakness now, and she was determined not to give in, not to—

His full mouth was so tantalizingly close, and her breath quickened as dull, familiar want began to tighten at her breasts, hot and heavy between her thighs. She licked her lips, and Akil swore softly under his breath, then stepped back.

"I told myself I wasn't here for that," he said as if trying to convince himself, then cleared his throat.

She found her lips tipping up despite herself. "We've never had any issues with that side of things, have we?"

"Certainly not." He tilted his dark head.

Tobi swallowed. He wasn't pressing her for a response, and she supposed that was something. Although a part of her, that deep dark bit she could not let surface, would not have minded at all if he pressed her hard against the tiled wall, lifted her skirt, acted on the possessive glimmer he was doing a poor job of hiding.

Akil had never been quite so afraid in his life, standing there in a freesia-and-vanilla-scented restroom lounge at the Chantilly Hotel, staring at Tobi's lovely face.

She wouldn't accept anything he did or said; why should she?

He'd managed to fall in love with the only person he'd treated terribly, and he had to reconcile that. Akil was not here because he expected Tobi to fall into his arms; that would be ridiculous, given all that he had done. But he wanted to tell her he was wrong, let her know on some level how much she meant to him. So he spoke.

"I think what I regret the most is the fact that I hurt you," he said. "My relationships are far more important than anything I've been chasing. And repairing mine with you is my first priority. I wronged you terribly, and I will spend the rest of my life trying to convince you to have faith in me, Tobi. In *us.*"

"You're not a man of faith."

"No." His eyes skimmed over her face. It looked thinner, and more tired than it had since he'd last seen it, and the thought that he was the one to cause those lines in that smooth skin...

"Tobi," he said. "My family is a study in self-ishness and in lack of care. It's all I saw growing up. My duty seemed the only thing worth fighting for, because there simply wasn't anything else." He took a breath. "But all I can think about now is you. You first, Tobi. I want to be precisely what you want. My duty is you, now. Us. And if what you said when we last saw each other is true, if it still stands—"

Here, he broke off. He could not speak any more, could not trust the words that came out of his mouth not to veer into his usual high-handed persuasion.

"I have very much to learn," he said humbly. "I'd just like some time to try."

"Akil, what are you saying?" Tobi asked, unwilling to allow herself to believe what she was hearing.

"I'm sorry," he said simply. "And I'd like you to come home."

Home. The word blurred her vision, just for a moment, and Akil began to speak again, looking deep into her eyes.

"Think about the way this city rose from the sand, how it came to be. Years of investment, decisions, work. Dedication. And if—"

He paused, and she tilted her head. "What?"

"I'm coming to see that love is like that," he said. "I was willing to work for Djoboro, but I wasn't willing to work for love. For you, although my heart was telling me otherwise. I blamed it on my father, and on my hatred for him. But Tobi, don't you see? If I do that, he *wins.* And I lose possibly the best thing I've ever had."

He stopped then, and crimson stained the copper of his skin. His eyes softened to the point that she blushed; the way he looked at her was more intimate than any caress, and she felt it so hard she pressed her hands to her stomach. He rested his forehead against hers.

"Tell me what you're thinking," Akil whispered, almost desperately. And then, sounding like his old self for the first time since he'd arrived, he added, "I insist."

"You can't force people to open up, Akil," she rebuked.

"No," he agreed. "So, then, what is it?"

She had to laugh, and she took a step back. "I want—I think I want you to take me back to my room."

Akil was kissing her now, safe in the innermost recesses of her suite at the Chantilly, and she could think of nothing else. His kisses were hard and hot and slick and a little brutal, and his breathing was low. Husky. He kissed her as if there was more of her below the surface of her mouth, and he was trying to reach it by all means. By the time his lips dropped warm and slow to that tender place on her neck to nip at the hollow where sweat already was collecting, Tobi was in danger of losing her footing.

"Please, Akil—I'm dizzy—"

"Good." There was a tense sort of satisfaction in those words, breathed low against her skin, and Tobi cried out as she felt herself hoisted upward as if she weighed nothing. Akil's hands were quick and impatient with her skirt and blouse, and in a flash, she felt herself lowered to her bed, and then Akil was looming over her. In the darkness of her room she could see nothing but the occasional flash of white that signified teeth or eyes; his hands seemed to be everywhere.

"I'm not here to force you," Akil said low, in her ear. The sound of his voice sent a ripple through her body that tensed it so violently she could not speak for a second. It wasn't fear or anger; it was want, the crippling sort of want that tightened her nipples to the point of pain, that caused that soft hidden place between her thighs to throb. It was Akil that had made her feel these things first; he was the only man who'd ever touched her like this. Who'd ever touched her at all, really.

"Akil," she ground out, and the tail end of a whimper came with it, for he was tracing a line from that hollow in her neck he'd kissed and bitten only moments ago down between her satin-covered breasts, over the quivering mound of her stomach, and lower—

He seemed to have gotten whatever confirmation he wanted, because she heard the soft rustling of clothing being removed, and he was in her bed. She fumbled for the bedside lamp, but she felt his grip lock lightly over her wrists, tug them upward.

"No," he said, and his long fingers were on

bare skin, skimming over a nipple so engorged and sensitive that she jumped. His fingers twisted hard round one flimsy strap till it broke; she started to protest, then choked instead as his mouth, hot and wet, closed over her breast. His other hand released its iron hold on her wrists and skimmed down between her thighs; they fell open eagerly, and she felt his surprise as he encountered soft skin and nothing else.

The feeling of his hands and mouth on her in the dark of her room was almost unbearably erotic; she was already beginning to shake. Akil withdrew his skillful fingers exactly at that point, and Tobi cramped almost painfully around nothing. She opened her mouth to protest, but was cut off again when the dress was wrenched down completely, and that slow, exploring mouth was descending her body.

Akil was speaking against her skin, low and filthy, a sort of gravelly huskiness in his voice. He said things that made her throat tighten, that made her heartbeat accelerate faster, as if that were possible. She was his, only his. He hadn't been able to sleep because she hadn't been there. He'd dreamed of her, and his body burned. His kisses were bruising, fierce; and Tobi rose to match him, meeting his passion with a fire of her own she had no idea she was capable of. *Mine*, he whispered in those final moments when he was buried deep in her silken heat when he finally let her shatter.

When dawn met them, naked, entwined and weary in the tangled sheets of Egyptian linen that covered the bed, Tobi squinted at her husband in the feeble light. Their fingers were laced together; his eyes were closed, and his chest rose and fell with each breath. He looked even more handsome in sleep, she thought. Her lips were still tender and bruised from his kisses as well as her own arousal; her breasts were heavy. Full. Swollen. Before she could ease herself from the bed Akil turned full over, reaching for her in his sleep, drawing her close to the warm scented folds of his body.

It felt so familiar, so *right*, that tears sprang to her eyes.

"I'm taking you home," he said, and there was a quiet desperation in his voice. "If you will come? I don't know how to do this, Tobi, how to not hold back."

"We both have a lot to learn." She hesitated. "It's a risk for me as well."

He was quiet for a moment. "Then I promise not to make you regret it. Tobi, I'm grateful I had the opportunity to fall in love with you. Goodness knows I didn't do anything to deserve it. And I will spend the rest of my days making sure you feel more loved and valued than you could have ever dreamed possible. That is, if you'll let me?" he asked.

This time, the tears that sprang to Tobi's eyes were of pure happiness. Akil loved her, truly loved her. And she believed him. The closed-off king had opened his heart to *her*. He'd shown her that she could do anything she set her mind to, and he was right.

"Yes, Akil. I'll let you," Tobi said with a growing smile. She pulled back and looked him in the eyes. "I love you, my king."

Akil smiled back, the biggest smile she'd ever seen. "And I love you, *my* queen."

EPILOGUE

One year later

THE HOUSE OF the king was indeed rebuilt, and it was truly beautiful.

Full of hopes and dreams for the future that quite eclipsed the uncertainty with which their relationship began, Akil and Tobi returned to Djoboro more reflective and a great deal wiser.

"We've much to work on, and some of it will be painful," Akil had said that first evening they were back, sitting shoulder to shoulder on the main balcony of their home. And it was, at first. There were tears. There were misunderstandings. There were tender moments, in which they pressed together so tightly it was difficult to tell where one began and the other ended. They cared for Jamila, who was finally coaxed into showing her grief, if only a little. They cared for the old king, and if Akil never was completely comfortable around him, at least he was back at the palace. He'd suffered, also, and was paying the ultimate price in the ruin of body, mind and spirit. And when the one-year celebration of Akil's ascension to the throne took place, the couple danced in the streets with their people with hearts that were as light as their feet.

Later that evening, arms wrapped round his neck in the quiet of his study, Tobi told Akil of her own dream.

"I haven't been to see anyone yet, but I'm fairly sure," she said softly, and laughed at the look of wonder on her husband's face. They'd talked about children, of course, in a sort of offhand way that indicated they would come eventually, but were not particularly planned for at the moment. To Tobi this felt all the more special; it had come so organically, from many nights of love.

Akil said nothing, and he didn't have to—the joy burning in his eyes was intense enough to consume them both. Instead Tobi bent, pressed her temple to his, and her mouth tipped upward as his hand skimmed the curve of her belly.

The little boy or girl to come in a few months' time would fill the corridors with laughter and gurgles, and give its parents joy for many years to come.

"I'm glad. I'm glad it's happening now," Tobi said after a moment. "We're ready for it now."

"I quite agree," Akil said, and kissed her gently.

The dancing princess and the rebel prince had finally found each other, and their future was as bright as the Djoboran sun.

* * * * *

If you enjoyed The Princess He Must Marry *you'll love the first installment in the Innocent Princess Brides duet* The Royal Baby He Must Claim *Available now!*

And don't miss Jadesola James's debut for Harlequin Presents Redeemed by His New York Cinderella